JESS A. MIELBICK

Blackbird

A Novel

ORGANICALLY
CRAFTED BOOKS

First published by Organically Crafted Books 2025

Copyright © 2025 by Jess A. Mielbick

This novel is entirely a work of fiction. The names, characters and incidents portrayed in it are the work of the author's imagination. Any resemblance to actual persons, living or dead, events or localities is entirely coincidental.

First edition

ISBN: 979-8-9992370-1-9

This book was professionally typeset on Reedsy.
Find out more at reedsy.com

For all the parents healing themselves
while trying to raise good humans.
You're doing a great job.

Prologue

30 years earlier

She lays in bed, resting uncomfortably on her lumpy second-hand mattress. The room is dark except for the nightlight, creating a yellow glow on the faux wood-paneled walls. Truly eighties-chic.

She is four years old, the age when some memories imprint in her brain while others slip away, like smoke disappearing after a candle burns out.

Muffled yells from the living room pierce through the walls. She often has trouble quieting her thoughts enough to sleep, especially on nights when she wakes to her parents' arguments.

Is this what it will be like when I grow up?

She pulls the birthday gift from her grandma off her shabby nightstand, a beautiful hand-painted jewelry box. Bright flowers frame its lid, a blackbird centered among them. She peels the purple ribbon from the top and opens the box again to hear its plinky song.

"Ding ding dingding dingding ding ding dinnng."

"No," she whispers into the dark. "It won't."

She quietly sings along with the music box until she finally drifts to sleep, the box held safely in her arms.

I

Trimester One

Eloise

January

Eloise stands in the aisle of the local drugstore, staring at all the brands of pregnancy tests. Her attention continuously shifts between the half-filled shelves and making sure that no one she knows is approaching the aisle. In such a small town, it's likely to happen, so she wants to hurry. The bright fluorescent lights reflect harshly off the row of optimistically pink boxes in front of her.

"Results up to 6 days before your missed period!"

"Two results, double confirmation!"

"Over 99% accurate!"

"Now with a longer handle and wider wick!"

There are other punctuation marks. Not everyone feels that level of excitement about this purchase.

As she scans the rows, her gaze rests for a moment on a box with a smiling, chubby-faced baby.

Eloise feels a quiet longing stir within her, one she's repressed too many times to count. She pulls her eyes away from the picture, reminding herself that she shouldn't bring more human beings into this already screwed up world.

With my luck and family history, I'd probably create the next Dahmer.

It took her a couple of weeks to even bring herself to the pharmacy. At first, she dismissed the nausea for a stomach bug.

She started feeling more tired and cranky.

Just PMS probably.

Then her breasts started hurting.

A new and concerning development...

She nervously checked her calendar.

I've been stressed lately. Maybe things are just running behind schedule... It's happened before.

But two weeks later, her period is still a no show.

As she stands in front of the boxes, shifting from one foot to the other, she still can't believe this is real. Her phone vibrates twice in her pocket.

Probably Parker.

If she's worried about being a mother, she's even more worried about Parker becoming a father right now...

The sound of approaching footsteps interrupts her thoughts and forces her back to the present. She quickly scans the boxes until she finds a white one with a simple blue design. Thankfully, it's also the cheapest. She snatches it from the shelf and hurries towards the checkout, wishing there was a self-checkout option. As she passes the cosmetics and toiletries, she grabs a few random items, an attempt to distract the cashier from the only item she really came here for.

Contact solution.

A bottle of vanilla scented lotion with a yellow Clearance sticker.

A package of multicolor disposable razors. The same ones she's been using since she was twelve.

She holds a box of ibuprofen, about to add it to her basket.

Wait, can I take this if...

The pills rattle as she puts it back on the shelf.

As she approaches the counter, she's relieved to see the apathetic teenage boy behind the register.

God bless him. He has the emotional range of a brick wall and won't make this situation more uncomfortable.

He lazily rings up the items and tells her the total. Eloise swipes her credit card, grabs her receipt and rushes from the store before he can even tell her to have the required "nice day."

Lucy

Lucy opens the visor to check her hair in the mirror. She carefully pats a few strays down around her severely chic bun, one of her three signature styles. She snaps the visor back into place as Allen backs his SUV out of their attached garage. He pulls away from the grayish green Craftsman before driving slowly through the quaint cul-de-sac they've called home for five years. Their neighbor is outside shoveling snow and Lucy waves to him as they pass.

Allen leans back comfortably in the driver's seat, while Lucy sits stiffly beside him. She looks out the passenger window, staring without really seeing.

Her playlist is on shuffle. Her taste is eclectic, and each artist defines a certain period of her life.

The catchy pop rock Panic! At the Disco song ends (her angsty teen era) and a folky song by The Beatles is up next (her wannabe hipster college years).

Lucy quietly sings along, her foot tapping slightly with nerves. Her thoughts are miles away from the music, though, and pinball from one anxiety to the next.

What if the test was wrong again? What if I'm not actually pregnant?

She won't allow herself to get her hopes up yet and instead thinks about their diminishing bank account.

We can't really afford treatments this time. Not when we're still paying off the ones from our first pregnancy.

Then it takes a darker turn, to thoughts she tries not to linger on or she risks having a panic attack.

What if there's something wrong with me instead? Something awful... What would happen to Allen and Drew? Would Drew even remember me if—

Allen interrupts her thoughts. "This song has always kind of bummed me out," he says.

"I love this song."

"I know you do." He glances towards her, but Lucy's gaze remains away from him. "You've never told me why."

Lucy sighs. "I'm not sure. There's always been something about it that resonated with me. I love that it's a little dark, but you still feel hopeful after you listen to it."

"You're so emo." Lucy hears his teasing tone, and finally looks away from the window. He smiles warmly at her. She smiles back, but is quick to reply with mock sass.

"Listen, I tell my students that music therapy is a valid practice, and this was my free therapy in college, okay?"

Snapshots of her college years briefly fill her mind. It took years of hard work (and more than a few tears) to get to where she is today- teaching part-time at the university and running her own private practice on the side. She can admit now that her career choice was a way for her to heal from her childhood, a very expensive way in hindsight. She stays though because she loves both her jobs, and lately they need the extra income after multiple failed rounds of fertility treatments that their insurance refused to cover.

"Okay, Dr. Green. If you say so." Her husband's eyes twinkle as he reaches for her hand. Despite his laid back attitude, Lucy can feel the slight moisture on his palms this morning.

She turns her head to see snow-covered trees pass, watching them sparkle in the bright sun. A mischievous smile plays on her lips.

"Speaking of therapy... I think I need some plant therapy today to help my stress levels. Can we stop at the garden center on our way back?" She keeps her gaze out the window, purposefully ignoring Allen this time. She can picture him turning towards her with an incredulous look on his face.

"Where the hell are you going to put another plant?!?" he asks.

She turns back to him. Sure enough, the facial expression she expected waits for her and she smiles.

"There's always room for another plant, babe. I haven't gotten a new one yet this year."

"It's not even a month into this year!" Allen protests. Lucy laughs and feels her anxiety for this appointment momentarily lessen.

Eloise

Eloise puts the test on the far side of the marbled laminate counter and sets a timer. Three minutes until she knows if her life will change forever. She doesn't want to look, but she can't stop from glancing at her phone screen every few seconds.

She puts a little concealer under her eyes to hide the dark circles.

What if it's positive?

She rubs it in.

Do I want it to be?

Then she reaches for her foundation.

It's going to be positive. I just know it.

She brushes the powder gently across her face and then closes the compact lid.

But am I really ready to raise a child?

This thought sets off a storm of practicalities she had no plans of considering anytime soon..

Where's the closest hospital that delivers babies?

Does my job offer maternity leave?

Can I buy a crib or stroller around here?

Does Babies "R" Us still exist?

How am I going to afford daycare?!?

She looks at the time.

Two minutes.

She grabs the eyeshadow pan and starts sweeping the shimmery brown powders across her lid. Her breathing quickens with her thoughts.

Even if I figure all that stuff out, what if I can't be a good mom? What if...

What if I can't give this baby a happier childhood than mine?

A wave of morning sickness hits her without warning.

Oh no, am I going to throw up?

No, don't throw up. Don't throw up.

Just stop thinking about it.

She focuses all her attention on her eyelids, blending the shadows together before digging through her cosmetic bag.

Where the hell is my mascara?

One minute.

The nausea passes and she breathes out in relief.

You don't HAVE to be a mom right now. There are other choices...

Partially remembered Bible quotes and sound bites of her childhood pastor fill her mind. The same longing she felt in the drugstore whispers behind these, but accepting it would require more honesty than Eloise is ready for right now. She's sure of one thing though.

If I am pregnant, I don't want to end it.

She swipes mascara across her eyelashes. Her hand is shaking slightly, so it makes it harder to not poke herself in the eye today.

There's adoption too.

Thirty seconds.

The longing gets louder. Her thoughts hover around it, but she still refuses to give it a permanent space.

What if I do that and he or she ends up having terrible parents?

She pictures a small child crying, eyes filled with fear. A figure looms darkly above, shouting and waving their arms aggressively.

Eloise can't stand to imagine this and shoves the images away. The need to protect the child reaches deep into her bones.

I want this baby.

Her hand pauses. She is inches from the mirror, forcing her to look herself closely in the eye. Resolve and confidence shine back at her. She isn't sure what to do with these unfamiliar feelings so she looks at the phone instead.

Ten seconds.

She puts her makeup back in the bag and tries to zip it closed. The zipper catches on the liner and she has to jiggle it free, tearing a piece of the lining off in the process.

"Dammit."

An instrumental, music box-like version of "Blackbird" starts playing on her phone.

The timer is going off.

Eloise closes her eyes and takes a deep breath.

Lucy

Lucy and Allen wait not-so-patiently in the recently updated fertility clinic. The smell of fresh paint makes Lucy a little nauseous, and she's cautiously optimistic that this is a good sign.

There's a knock on the door and her reproductive endocrinologist enters.

"Hi, how are you guys?"

"Nervous," Lucy answers honestly.

Allen gently puts his hand on her back. She can feel the slightest trembling in his fingertips against her black turtleneck sweater. Lucy looks closely at the doctor, trying to assess the type of news she's about to hear. She's had enough appointments with Dr. Smythe to recognize some of her nonverbal cues.

I could probably beat her in poker.

If I actually knew how to play.

"Well, I think I can help with that." Dr. Smythe sits down on her stool, rolls it a few inches closer to them, and smiles. Lucy's heart flutters hopefully. "I got your blood work back and you're pregnant."

Happy tears fill Lucy's eyes. Allen beams at her and rubs her back a little harder.

Lucy tries talking, but her voice is too thick with emotion. She clears her throat. "That's amazing. I was so worried this wouldn't happen for us again, at all."

Dr. Smythe smiles back at them, her eyes a little more glossy than when she first walked into the room.

"I'm so happy for you both. These are my favorite appointments." Though her demeanor remains professional, her voice wavers slightly. "We'll table your treatment plan. You can schedule your first ultrasound when you leave and we'll go from there. Do you have any questions?"

"No, I think we're good. Thank you so much."

Dr. Smythe smiles at them again.

"Congrats, you two. Take a minute and leave whenever you're ready. See you in a couple of weeks."

Allen looks at Lucy as the doctor leaves the room, his eyes wet.

"I guess we can stop so you can get another plant, but only because it's a celebratory one."

She laughs and cries harder as he pulls her in for a hug. She feels a familiar sadness dilute her joy when she thinks about how she wishes she could tell her mom the news.

Eloise

She opens her eyes slowly. Eloise shuts off the timer and takes one more steadying breath.

Stop procrastinating. You already know what it's going to say.

She slides her eyes across the countertop to look at the test and as anticipated, two pink lines stare confidently back at her. The lines blur and she's surprised that tears have filled her eyes. She rarely cries.

Must be the pregnancy hormones.

Pregnant…. Her.

She smiles and a small, shaky laugh escapes her.

You're having a baby.

An actual baby.

That you will be responsible for raising.

She grabs a tissue to wipe her eyes, careful that she doesn't smudge her makeup. She hears the bedroom door creak open and her smile fades.

How will Parker feel…?

Anytime she's tried bringing up having children he always says something like, "It's too soon to talk about that" or "I don't want them right now." She didn't force the issue because at the time she agreed with him. They didn't *need* to talk about it. Then…

She quietly forces the test to the bottom of the Walmart bag lining the trash can, making sure it's fully covered. She crumples one more tissue on top before leaving the bathroom.

Eloise walks to the kitchen and sees Parker standing in front of the coffeepot with puffy eyes and a bad case of bedhead. He fills the largest mug she owns with steaming coffee, leaving a small cup for her in the pot.

He barely glances at her as he turns around to sit at the dining table.

"Morning," he says gruffly. Eloise stares at the back of his messy head and broad shoulders, wishing he'd pull her into one of his warm hugs or even give her a light kiss on the cheek like he used to every morning.

What happened to the charming guy I met two years ago? I haven't seen him in months.

She turns around to pour herself some coffee.

He used to get this for me every morning.

She sees a line of empty beer cans on the counter.

And that Parker didn't drink a six pack every weeknight...

"Do you want a ride to work this morning?" Eloise asks as she adds creamer to her mug.

"No."

"It's kind of icy out. Are you sure you don't want me to drop you off?"

"I said no."

Take that ray of sunshine and walk yourself there then.

She opens the refrigerator to return the creamer and gently says, "Your lunch is on the top shelf here."

"Thanks," Parker mumbles so that Eloise barely hears him.

She shakes her head and rolls her eyes behind his back.

If he can't afford a car, how can he afford a baby...

She clears her throat and glances at him to better assess his mood.

"I was hoping we could talk about something tonight. I'm making chicken burritos."

His favorite.

"I won't be home for dinner. I'm going to my brother's to watch the game."

"Oh, okay."

There goes that plan.

"Maybe we can go out to dinner this weekend?"

Parker stands up abruptly and dumps the remainder of his coffee down the drain.

"Maybe."

Eloise watches him walk to the bathroom until his back disappears behind the door. She sighs deeply.

At least I'm not still wasting money and time on dating apps.

What a bonus.

She tries to think of Parker's old profile.

He answered the question about kids as "maybe."

Right...?

Yes, he must have, or I wouldn't have reached out to him.

She finishes her coffee, feeling some of her earlier confidence return.

Lucy

February

Lucy's toddler son, Drew, stands on a chair at their kitchen counter wearing a checkered teal apron. Lucy stands beside him wearing a matching adult-sized version. Flour, sugar, butter, spices, and other ingredients lay on the quartz countertop in a haphazard, but easily accessible manner. Lucy carefully cracks two eggs into a large metal mixing bowl.

Super thankful I haven't developed any aversions to baking so far in this pregnancy.

"Okay, mix the eggs," Lucy instructs.

Her son's small arms frantically stir the beginning of the banana bread batter, her grandmother's special recipe.

"Like this?"

She smiles as she watches him. "Yup. Just like that. I'll peel the bananas while you do that."

She puts them on a plate and hands Drew a fork.

"Do you want to mash them?"

"Yeah!" Drew grabs the fork and enthusiastically presses it into the fruit. Pieces of mashed banana fly around and land on the cabinet in front of her, leaving white specks on the dark navy paint. She wipes them up as she pulls the mixing bowl closer.

"Great job, buddy. Let's put the bananas in the bowl now and stir it all together."

Drew starts stirring, slowing down as the batter becomes thicker.

"How about you do it?"

"Sure, bud. Is your arm getting tired?"

She takes the spoon from him and starts mixing the batter.

"Wow! You so fast!" He looks at her in childlike wonder.

"Someday when your muscles are bigger, you can mix it fast, too."

Drew watches her, then puts his hand sweetly around her back to rest it there and asks, "Okay, what next?"

Between the small weight of his arm and his K's said as T's, she can't help smiling as she reaches for the next ingredient. These quiet moments in the kitchen with Drew remind her of all the times she baked with her grandmother. She feels the usual sadness and guilt creep into the edges of her thoughts.

My children won't have the same experience with my mom.

Unexpectedly, her vision shimmers. She looks down and instead of the mixing bowl in front of her, she clearly sees her hands on a steering wheel and a snow covered road in front of her. She blinks and the bowl is back.

Oh no. Not again.

Drew's quiet singing breaks through her thoughts.

"Peanut. Peanut butter. And jelly!"

She wrinkles her brows as she tries to remember the lyrics of the song to see the connection he's made.

"Then you take the peanuts and you mash them, you mash them."

She smiles. *Got it.*

She glances at Drew's smiling face, thankful that she can make these memories with him. Her greatest hope is that the good ones are the ones he remembers clearest, and not the moments she's acting like an overstimulated porcupine. She pushes the icy images out of her mind for now.

"Okay. I think we're about done, buddy." She looks at the flour and batter splattered across the counter. "Whoa. We made a mess."

"What a mess! I clean it!"

Drew grabs for the paper towel roll in front of him.

He looks at her with wide and serious eyes.

"We need a lot of paper towel." He pulls three sheets towards himself.

With mom-speed, Lucy stops the roll and pulls off one towel. "I think one should be enough."

"Okay..."

Drew smears batter around the counter and Lucy purses her lips slightly. She hears her mom's distant voice, like it's coming through a dense fog.

"Since you aren't going to, I guess I'll clean that up too."

Lucy blinks and shakes her head.

A little mess is not a big deal, and he's a toddler.

They're naturally messy.

And there's lots of research to support messy play for healthy development.

So chill, Porcupine.

"Do you want to play with Magnatiles after we put the bread in the oven?"

"Yeah!" Drew doesn't wait and scrambles down from the chair. He pulls the mini apron off his head as he runs and drops it behind him.

"I'll just finish up by myself then, huh?" Lucy hears the bin of tiles clatter to the ground in the living room. She takes a deep breath and wipes up the kitchen.

Eloise

Eloise drives her just-beginning-to-rust sedan slowly, stuck behind a long line of traffic. She taps her fingers on the wheel with growing irritation.

Par for the fricken' course this week.

Two days ago her next-door neighbor's large tree branch fell into Eloise's backyard, and she assumes they have no intention of cleaning it up. Now she has one more problem to figure out. She's had to scrape snow and ice off her car three days in a row and yesterday on the way out, she hit her elbow on the front door jamb, hard enough to cause her eyes to water. To add insult to injury, now the door doesn't latch right.

So, of course, it makes sense that today she gets stuck in traffic on her way to work, traffic being a tractor taking up one and a half lanes with a line of cars trailing behind it. Even without the tortoise-like farm equipment, vehicles are moving slowly on the slushy roads. She sighs with annoyance.

Thankfully, she only works one town away. She left early to avoid seeing Parker before he woke up, so she shouldn't be late anyway. Eloise hates being late.

Ironic right now, really.

She watches in her rear view mirror as a car races toward her and then passes her. It drives past the car in front of her and the car in front of that. Then finally it speeds past the tractor, barely missing the oncoming car in the opposite lane as it slides back onto the right side of the road.

"Idiot," she breathes out and shakes her head.

She changes the radio station and finds the pop station she's listened to since high school. It's transitioning to an "oldies" station lately. She should care that she is now considered "old" to today's youth, but she likes the nostalgia of hearing songs from when she was younger. The hosts are in the middle of taking calls and reading messages for today's morning question:"If you never had to work another day in your life, how would you spend your time?"

"Travel the world."

"Work on my photography skills."

"Crochet."

"Write a book."

"Have too many pets."

"Chase sunrises and sunsets."

Privileged dreamers.

She stopped letting herself think outside her own reality a long time ago, and if she's honest with herself, she was never very good at it when she was younger either.

She finally reaches the parking lot of her office building and pulls into a spot. She exits her car and passes by the faded business sign that hangs outside the double doors. Some letters in *Frank Accounting* are missing, but nobody sees the point in fixing it. Everyone in town knows what the business is and there aren't extra funds for cosmetic fixes even if they wanted to upgrade.

She enters the beige, outdated office and sits down at the reception desk, placing her lunch on the far right side like she does every day. She turns on the computer and switches the phones over from their automated message.

"Good morning, Eloise," Sarah says as she walks in, stopping at Eloise's desk for their typical morning chat.

"Morning, Sarah."

"How are you today?"

"Good."

Sarah's brow wrinkles slightly. She stares at Eloise closely, quickly picking up on her irritated mood. "Yeah? You seem tired today. Are you feeling okay?"

"Yes, I'm fine."

Perk up a little. Don't hurt her feelings.

Eloise smiles at Sarah tightly.

Leave it to her closest friend in the office (and honestly in her life) to pick up that something is different today. Eloise has always thought that Sarah has a sixth sense or something.

"Are we having lunch together today?" Sarah asks.

"Yes, looking forward to it." Eloise turns back to her desk and starts shuffling papers around to end the conversation quicker.

Sarah walks away, but as she does, she looks over her shoulder at Eloise again, unconvinced by her charade.

I can't tell her before I tell Parker. It wouldn't be fair to him.

Eloise catches Sarah's eye and smiles again, forcing it a little brighter this time. She'll have to work on her lying skills if she's going to make it through lunch without her secret tumbling out.

Lucy

While the bread bakes, Lucy feels nauseous and barely makes it to the bathroom in time. Drew continues to play quietly, thankfully oblivious that Lucy left him.

She washes her hands and yawns. She didn't forget the morning sickness, but she forgot how tiring the first trimester can be. When she was pregnant with Drew, she could nap after work. Now she doesn't have that luxury. She looks at herself in the bathroom mirror and sees heavy bags under her eyes. Her shoulders and neck are tight too and she can feel a headache coming on.

It hardly seems fair that our bodies don't allow us nine months to rest before being expected to take care of the human equivalent of a gremlin.

She washes and dries her hands. A calendar reminder to pay the mortgage scrolls across her phone screen just as she hears the timer go off in the kitchen.

"Mom! Mom! Beeeeep!"

She's pushing a few stray hairs back into the knot at the base of her neck when Drew enters the bathroom. She glimpses his reflection in the mirror as he lifts himself up to hang from the curtain behind her.

"Stop!"

She turns quickly as the curtain, rod and her son crash to the floor. She sees the gaping hole left in the drywall and she's instantly filled with an intense, impulsive rage.

"Dammit! How many times do I have to tell you not to do that?" she yells. She sees Drew's eyes fill, first with fear and then with tears.

She takes a deep breath. Her tone is still sharp, but she tries to soften it as she says, "I need you to leave for a minute so I can calm down."

He runs from the room crying, heavy guilt now matching her anger.

Way to go, Mom of the F-ing Year.

She takes a second deep breath, heart still pounding.

It's just a wall. It's fixable.

She feels nauseous again, but knows it isn't morning sickness this time. This feeling is all too familiar for her liking. It's never in the initial moment she remembers to check her short temper, and she always responds a second too late.

Just like my father.

She pictures his intimidating figure coming toward her.

Sees her small frame crouching down.

Trying to make herself as small as possible.

Trying to disappear.

You don't want your kid to walk on eggshells like you had to.

She walks softly into the living room where her son is sitting on the floor by the Magnatiles again.

She quietly sits down beside Drew, visually checking to see if he looks physically hurt.

"Are you okay, hun?" Drew rubs tears from his eyes and avoids looking at her. "Did you get hurt, or were you just scared?"

"Scared." His bottom lip pouts. Her heart breaks that she is the cause of his current emotions, and her eyes begin to water.

"I'm sorry I got angry with you. I was mad about what happened, but I shouldn't have yelled at you."

He still doesn't look at her. She moves closer to him, desperate to restore their connection.

"I'm sorry, buddy. Come here."

Drew crawls into her lap, and she wraps him in a big hug. He wipes his eyes on her shirt and sniffles into her chest, but she can tell he's calming down.

"Uh oh… here comes the tickle monster!"

Her son's reluctant giggles fill the room.

"Stop, Mama."

"Alright. Are you okay?"

"I okay."

She gives him another quick squeeze and a kiss on the cheek.

"I love you, Drew."

Drew sniffs the air.

"What I smell?"

Lucy sniffs too.

"I don't know. It smells like something is... Oh no! The bread!"

Eloise

Eloise glances at the clock and sees it's nearly lunchtime, finally. The phone hasn't rung in hours, and she filed the stack of papers waiting for her in the first hour of her day. Now she passes the time by doodling on a sticky note. Wildflowers dance along the edges, forming a frame. Inside the frame is a landscape of a meadow. She feels less irritable than she did this morning.

"Ready to eat?" Eloise looks up, surprised she hadn't heard Sarah approach.

She quickly covers the note with the first piece of paper she can grab, but not before Sarah sees it.

"You're so talented, Eloise."

Eloise breaks eye contact and ignores Sarah's comment. She quickly stands and grabs her lunch bag. "Let's go eat. I'm starving."

They walk to the empty break room. A half empty coffee pot sits on the burner. It smells like stale coffee and Eloise stifles a gag.

"Actually, I think the conference room is empty. Would you mind eating there today?"

"Sure..." Sarah looks at her curiously.

"How was your weekend? I forgot to ask," Eloise says as they sit down at the large table. They shift some discarded papers and boxes aside to make room.

"Oh, it was good. Went shopping with my mom and then saw a movie with Matt. How about you? You didn't tell me what you did."

"Nothing much. I wasn't feeling great, so I took it easy. Read a little. Napped. Caught up on some cleaning."

Definitely didn't pee on a stick and learn my entire life was about to change...

As if reading her thoughts, Sarah bluntly asks, "You're pregnant, aren't you?"

Eloise nearly spits out a mouthful of water. She chokes and needs a minute to reply.

"Shit, Sarah! Why would you ask that?"

"Something's off with you, between the gag you just tried hiding, the dark circles under your eyes and you going to the bathroom five times this morning. Am I right?"

Eloise looks down and replies quietly, "Yes."

Sarah's eyes soften. "How are you feeling?"

"Tired and nauseous."

"Sure, but I meant emotionally. I assume this is... unexpected...?"

"Oh no, I definitely planned this. Seemed like a fantastic way to add some excitement to my boring life." Eloise gives a short sarcastic laugh before the wrinkle returns between her eyebrows. "It doesn't really seem real. I don't know how to feel yet."

Scared. Terrified actually.

And lonely.

The excitement she felt after seeing the lines on the test hasn't left her though, even if she doesn't really want to be in this situation right now. Sarah interrupts her thoughts.

"How did Parker take the news?"

Eloise shifts in her seat uncomfortably. "Um... he... I..."

"You haven't told him?"

"The timing hasn't felt right."

Sarah raises her eyebrow and Eloise sighs, "Okay, and I don't know how. I'm worried about what he'll say."

"Do you want me to be there with you?" Eloise hears softness in Sarah's voice but cannot meet her eyes. She pushes her salad around with her fork.

"No. I can do it. I just need a few days to think about it."

Sarah gently touches her arm, forcing Eloise to look up at her. Sincerity and kindness fill her eyes and voice as she says, "You can do this. Call me if you need anything, please."

Eloise smiles back at her, comforted by her friend's support. "Thanks, Sarah."

Lucy

Every time Lucy looks at the hole in her bathroom wall, she's reminded of her reaction, and she relives the shame and guilt she felt for yelling at Drew.

If I'm already this tightly wound with one kid, what happens when we have another one?

On her way to the coffee shop today, she called their contractor to see if he could stop in soon to patch the drywall and reinstall the curtain rod for them. She adds the date and time they agreed on to her calendar while she waits for her drink. As she presses "Save" the barista slides a glass across the bar.

"Iced dirty chai latte with oat milk and cold foam."

Lucy steps up to the counter, well aware this order is one adjective away from her needing to buy a Gucci handbag.

She finds a table to wait for her sister, Bree. She's about to set her phone down but then sees a notification from daycare. Lucy opens it to a picture of Drew playing outside. He's smiling at the camera as he drives a Cozy Coupe through the snowy play yard. Lucy smiles and saves it to her photo gallery.

He isn't wearing his gloves.

She's about to send a message to the staff but stops herself.

He's fine. They're taking care of him.

Deep breath, Mama Bear.

She closes the daycare app and taps her library one instead. Bree is historically late to their monthly dates, and most events, for that matter, so Lucy figures she has a few minutes to read the psychological thriller that's this month's book club pick. It was Margaret's month to host and when Lucy thinks about her sweet, elderly friend and her surprising love for thrillers,

31

she smirks.

There's a fire crackling in the corner and music plays softly from the speakers. The busy espresso machine adds to the white noise.

She's just gotten to the part where the honeymooning couple discovers they aren't alone on the island (*Of course, when are they ever alone in these books?*) when she sees her sister breeze into the cafe. Bree waves at her and smiles. She eases her way around the other tables to reach Lucy's. Snowflakes lightly cover her heavy wool coat, and a few twinkle in her hair from the cafe's warm lights.

"Hey! How are you?" Bree says once she's within talking distance.

"Good. How are you?"

"Great. I'm going to get a drink and I'll be right back." Bree drops her bag into the chair and pulls out her wallet before heading to the counter.

She orders and then comes back to wait for her drink. She sees Lucy's glass and wrinkles her nose.

"Iced coffee when it's this cold out? I haven't seen you drink iced coffee in the winter since you were pregnant with Drew."

Lucy raises her eyebrows meaningfully.

"Wait... are you?!?" Bree's eyes widen with hope and excitement. She knows how frustrated Lucy has been by their fertility issues.

A smile breaks out across Lucy's face. "Yes."

"Awww, Lucy! I'm so happy for you." Bree stands back up and moves quickly around the table to give Lucy a hug that only Bree can give. Her order is called, and she grabs it from the counter before returning to her seat.

"That secret didn't last long," Lucy says.

"Can't hide anything from me, sis. When are you due?"

"October."

"Perfect, your birthday month! Ahh, I'm so excited for you guys!"

Lucy continues smiling as she sips her drink. "Thanks. We're excited too. I'm just so thankful it's finally happening for us again."

"I bet." Bree's eyes soften sympathetically but remain bright with enthusiasm. "How have you been feeling?"

"Okay. The morning sickness has already started. I don't care how many times the doctor tells me that's a good sign. It sucks."

Bree laughs. "Seriously. Pregnancy is actually kind of the worst… If we could have babies without all the negative parts of pregnancy, I'd have ten more kids."

"Speaking of kids, how are Liam and Miles?"

"Great! We'll have to get together soon. Miles has been asking when he can come play with Drew."

"Maybe dinner on Sunday?"

They set a tentative time and move on to discuss work.

Lucy feels a sense of pride as her younger sister talks about how she's balancing her full-time job while working towards her MBA.

Someone has to be excited for her. Lord knows our parents couldn't care less about our accomplishments.

With this thought, Lucy sips from her straw before initiating a semi-regular conversation topic. Her chest tightens, and she unconsciously stretches her shoulders back in response.

"Have you heard from Mom or Dad in awhile?"

"Nope," Bree replies with her usual answer. "Must be too busy with their new lives to care about reminders from their old one."

The fire crackles. A cold draft of air passes over them as the door opens to let in more customers.

"It feels weird that they don't even know about Drew and now this baby, too. But I also don't want them to know anything about them, you know?"

Bree nods understandingly. Lucy absentmindedly stirs her drink, ice clinking quietly against the glass.

"Don't you wish they'd reach out, though?" She raises her eyes to look at Bree, uncertainty hanging from her words.

Bree answers, a thoughtful look on her face. Her tone remains light, but some of her usual enthusiasm is missing from her eyes.

"No, not anymore. I used to, but I got so sick of waiting that now I don't care. Well, I mean, I DO care, but… You know what I mean."

Lucy nods slowly.

But do I really?

I could reach out to them too and I feel like a huge B-I-T-C-H that I don't.

Lucy tightens the clip holding back half her hair, the closest she gets to leaving it down.

"I was just thinking the other day about how sad it is that my kids won't have the same relationship with their grandparents that we had with ours." Lucy pictures Drew's sweet face as she stares down at her glass.

"I know. I think about that a lot, too." Bree raises her cup to her mouth, blowing on it to cool it. "My kids also can't play with play dough without me wanting to freak the F out on them when they mix colors, though."

"Talk about learned behavior, babe." Lucy smiles, but sadness reflects in her eyes. "After all these years, I still can't believe they walked away without even trying to change. Makes me feel real good about myself, very loved."

She laughs half-heartedly and her sister joins in.

"It's amazing we turned out as well as we did," Bree says.

"Seriously."

Bree's phone rings and she glances down at it.

"Shoot. It's the school." She stands up and walks outside to answer it. She's gone less than a minute before she bustles back inside.

"I have to go. Liam threw up in Gym. We may have to reschedule for Sunday."

"Yeah, please don't bring that garbage into my house. I'm already throwing up enough. Just let me know."

"I will. Congrats, Luce. So happy for you guys." Bree pulls her in for another hug and then grabs her cup off the table. "See you later!"

"Bye. Hope Liam feels better!"

"Thanks! Me too! Love you!"

Her sister walks away before Lucy has the chance to reply. She's relieved because even though her sister is one of the most important people in her life and Lucy loves her deeply, saying the actual words still feels unnatural to her.

Lucy consciously deepens her breathing as she watches her sister leave. She takes one final deep breath and checks the time.

One more hour until I have to be back at the office.

She takes another drink of her bougie beverage and readjusts the scarf tucked around her neck. She opens her phone and returns to the unfortunate honeymooning couple.

Eloise

Parker and Eloise are sitting at the yellow Formica dining table she bought at the thrift store a couple of years ago. Faint scratches mark the top, but she fell in love with it and couldn't leave it there.

Parker's eyes are glued to his phone. "God dammit! The Packers lost. There goes the Super Bowl."

Eloise continues eating her dinner without looking up, deciding that silence may be the safest choice right now. She wipes the spaghetti sauce from the corner of her mouth.

More than a week has passed since Sarah discovered her secret and Eloise knows she should already have told Parker. She's been so tired after work every night that she didn't have the energy to even start the conversation though. She planned on doing it over the weekend, but when Parker wasn't miserably grumpy or at his brother's, he was drinking.

Just never found the right moment to drop that bomb.

She was going to tell him tonight, but now doesn't seem like the best time either. He's been cranky since he got home from work.

Maybe later while he's watching TV.

She eats another bite of pasta while Parker takes his empty plate to the sink and sets it inside.

It would be easier if he would just open the dishwasher that's half a foot away and put it in there instead.

She isn't about to suggest that to him, especially not tonight, and she's never been comfortable sharing her thoughts and feelings, even to herself.

She hears a can pop open and watches as Parker goes into the living, puts

36

his feet up on the coffee table and turns on the television.

Perfect. The Simpsons will make him less grumpy.

Maybe I'll offer him a bowl of ice cream later, too.

She goes into the kitchen and places both their dishes in the dishwasher, scoops the leftovers into containers and sets them in the fridge.

Her phone rings and "Mom" flashes on the screen.

She sighs heavily before answering.

"Hey, Mom."

"Hey, hun! How are you?"

"Fine. How are you?"

"Oh, you know. Your dad is giving me a headache."

She listens for the next ten minutes as her mom complains to her about her dad and all his wrongs. She's been out of the house for fifteen years and it's like she never left. It's the same conversation they've had a thousand times before.

"Oh, that reminds me." Her mom suddenly shifts topics, regaining Eloise's full attention. "I saw Janet Decker last week. She looks so old! I can't believe it."

"Oh really? Well, she's probably in her late sixties now."

Eloise didn't realize until she was an adult how her mother rarely had anything positive to say about others. Or herself. Or life.

Did she complain to me, or worse, about me, when I was a kid?

Eloise tries to remember, but she feels a headache of her own brewing. She hears Parker laugh in the next room and thinks now might be the best time to talk to him.

Time to rip off the bandage.

"Mom, I have to go. I'll talk to you later, okay?"

"Okay. Wait! Are you coming to dinner on Sunday?"

"Sure. Do you want me to bring anything?"

"No, I think I have it covered. It would be nice if your dad would pitch in every once in a while, though."

"Yeah… It would. I'll see you Sunday and I'll bring some rolls."

Eloise says goodbye, puts her phone in her pocket and pours herself some water. She calls into the living room, "Do you want some ice cream?"

"Absolutely."

She scoops Parker some before sitting down beside him on the couch.

"This is a good episode," he says, smiling widely at her, mouth full of ice cream.

She sits quietly and sips her water while he takes a long gulp of his beer. Her stomach turns over at his food and drink combination.

He leans over, kisses her cheek and hands her his empty can. "Hey babe, can you get me another one?"

"Sure." She stands up, and he slaps her butt as she walks by him. She cringes inside but says nothing.

Don't set him off again...

When she comes back, he cracks open the can and puts his arm around her shoulders. His warmth does little to comfort her tonight.

Just get it over with. When the next commercial comes on, tell him then.

A familiar jingle for a used car dealership starts the commercial break.

Damn. That was quick.

She takes in a deep breath, trying to steady herself, and forces her toe to stop bouncing.

"Hey. I have something to tell you."

"Uh oh." Parker's eyes twinkle like they used to as he looks down at her. Then he sees her serious face, and it dissolves again.

"What? What is it?" he asks aggressively.

She replies quieter this time. "Um... I'm... pregnant."

"What?! God fucking dammit!"

He stands up unexpectedly, forcing Eloise forward as the weight of his arm leaves her shoulders. Beer sloshes from the can and lands on the coffee table in front of her.

"Are you fucking kidding me? How the hell did this happen, Eloise?"

She looks down at her hands twisting in her lap.

Parker yells a little quieter this time, "I thought you were taking care of it!"

"I did. I took my pills every day. I don't know how it happened."

"Well, that doesn't really matter now, does it? I don't want a goddamn kid.

What the hell are we supposed to do?"

"I don't know," she answers timidly.

"Well, I don't know either, but you better figure it out."

What is there to figure out?

She breathes in deeply, searching for even a sliver of confidence. When she speaks, Eloise's voice is barely above a whisper.

"I'm keeping the baby."

Parker stills and stares at her, measuring her up. He shakes his head and says with a hint of disgust, "Of course you are. Why not ruin our lives?"

He throws the beer can onto the coffee table before walking to the door and yelling one last, "Shit!"

The door slams and Eloise sits back defeated, ashamed, alone... She sighs before standing up to get a towel for the mess.

Guess his dating profile should have said, "Not interested in having kids." Now I know.

She feels her throat tighten as she returns the towel to the kitchen. A sob bursts out and she grips the counter tightly.

Stupid hormones.

Lucy

Lucy starts every day by eating crackers in bed to stop herself from throwing up, but it only works about half the time. Today is one that it didn't, and she's struggling to make it through her Child and Adolescent Psychology class. Fifty pairs of eyes stare back at her as she takes deep breaths, waiting for her to continue the lesson.

Don't throw up. Don't throw up.

She nudges the small trash can she's stashed under the desk to make it more accessible if she needs it.

But you won't need it.

She clicks her presentation, and a black-and-white image of a mustached, kind-looking gentleman appears. She shifts the peppermint in her mouth before speaking.

"Erik Erikson was a developmental psychologist famous for his theory on psychosocial development."

Lucy clicks through her slideshow. Halfway through the lecture, she looks out at the class and sees some students are taking diligent notes, while others' eyes have already glazed over.

There's about to be more glaze in here than at a Krispy Kreme.

At the tiniest thought of donuts, her nausea intensifies. She takes a long breath in through her nose.

Just keep going.

She breathes out slowly, clicks again. The first tier of a chart flashes and then stays lit.

"I've been working on my tech skills." Lucy looks at the class, her eyes wide with exaggerated excitement. A few students chuckle to humor her.

Lucy smiles, momentarily distracted from the churning in her stomach. She clicks through all the stages and makes sure to sarcastically point out the outdated and lackluster animation.

Almost there.

She clicks again and "Summary" zooms onto the screen like a racecar. Lucy recaps the lesson before clicking one final time.

Click. "Homework" bounces onto the screen like a ball.

Finally.

"I went a little old school with this one. This was my favorite animation when I was in elementary school. You know, a hundred years ago when computers were first created." She sees some students smile while others roll their eyes. "Make sure you read chapter ten before our next class. See you next time and make good choices."

Students bustle from the room after her closing catchphrase. She loves her students, but thankfully no one stays after to ask questions.

Lucy grabs her laptop and stuffs it into her bag. She quickly exits the room and makes a beeline for the nearest bathroom, knowing she has only a moment to get there. She's so focused she nearly bumps into her colleague, Angela.

"Hey, Lucy! How are you?"

"I'm okay."

"You don't look so great… Are you sick?" Angela takes in her sweaty, pale appearance.

"I'm actually not feeling well. I'll talk to you later!"

She leaves Angela staring after her. Angela seems unsure if she should follow, likely wanting to make sure that Lucy is ok. Lucy prays she doesn't. The last thing she wants is an audience.

* * *

Their entry door opens, the beginning of a creak barely audible.

We'll have to put something on the hinges.

"Dada! Hugsie!"

Drew tosses his crayon onto the counter and hops off the bar stool.

"Careful!" Lucy yells to him, turning quickly to catch him.

Drew lands lightly on the floor though and then skids through the kitchen to greet his dad.

"Hey, buddy! How are you?"

Allen closes the door from the garage and scoops Drew up for a bear hug.

"Good. I play with Everett at school."

"Fun! What did you play?"

"Monster Trucks!"

"Awesome!" He looks over Drew's head to talk to Lucy. "Do you want me to finish dinner?"

"No, I'm almost done. Thanks for offering."

"Okay." He turns back to Drew. "Want to play with cars in the living room?"

"Yeah!"

"Okay. Go get them out and I'll be right there." Allen sets Drew down and he races out of the room.

Allen turns to Lucy and places his hand on her back. He leans in and kisses her cheek as she continues cooking grilled cheese sandwiches for dinner. It's one of the few things that doesn't make her sick just thinking about it. She at least used fancier Italian bread and smoked Gouda to make the meal feel a little more grown up.

"How was your day?"

"Fine. Threw up again at work."

"Gross."

"Tell me about it. How was your day?"

"Fine. Kind of slow and boring today."

"Dada!"

"I didn't throw up at least," Allen chuckles as he heads into the living room to play with their son.

She calls after him, "Count yourself lucky then!" Lucy finishes putting dinner on their plates, cutting cucumber and strawberries for Drew and a side salad for her and Allen. Tonight's to-do list runs through her mind.

The laundry needs to get folded.

I still need to pack Drew's lunch for daycare tomorrow.

Ugh, and I need to finish grading those tests. They've been sitting there all week.

I'll ask Allen to fold the laundry so I can finish them.

And have him find the WD-40 for the door. I probably shouldn't spray that while pregnant.

She calls into the living room a few minutes later, "Dinner's ready."

She hears Allen say to Drew, "Let's clean up the cars and then go eat."

The sound of cars haphazardly being tossed back into their basket reaches her ears. She smiles as Allen says, "Let's put them nicely in the basket, bud."

That's a phrase I'd say.

When they're done, Drew races back into the dining room and climbs into his chair. He looks down at his plate to see what he's having tonight.

"Yum! Strawberries!"

He puts a chunk in his mouth and grins at Lucy, his eyes crinkling, cheeks bulging like a chipmunk's.

She smiles back and thinks about how lucky she is before feeling another wave of nausea approaching.

I wish I could stop throwing up, though. I'd get a lot more done every day.

Eloise

On Sunday, Parker drives Eloise to her parents' house for dinner. The roads are snow covered, but it's a short drive. Like her mother and grandmother, Eloise has always lived within twenty miles of where she grew up.

Parker's hands are tight on the steering wheel, the muscles in his jaw tense. He's looked this way since she told him she was pregnant. Eloise feels a familiar tension in her own shoulders. The closer they get to her family's house, the tighter they feel, like they do every time she returns to her childhood home.

Their conversation for the entire drive is minimal. She's been especially cautious around him since her failed announcement.

Maybe sports would break the ice... That's a safe topic.

"I bet Dad would love to watch the game with you."

Parker ignores her. She lets a few more minutes pass.

Or food. They say a way to a man's heart is through his stomach, right?

"My mom said she's making a chicken dinner." No response. "With all the sides."

Silence.

Forget it then.

Instead of trying to find a different topic, she silently looks out the car window and notes the subtle changes over the last two decades- new siding on a house here, a closed business there.

She remembers riding in her friends' cars, driving on these same roads and listening to them talk about their post-high school plans. She thinks about why she stayed here- lack of family support, finances, fear...

44

A two-story colonial she's never seen before passes by her window. She turns to look at it again and it's no longer there. Instead, it's replaced with the empty cornfield she was expecting.

That was...weird.

She doesn't mention this to Parker. She isn't even sure what she would say.

"Hey, did you see that house, or am I imagining things?"

They pull into her parents' gravel driveway with Eloise still feeling confused. Smoke from the chimney billows into the cold air above the faded gray ranch. Her mom meets them at the door.

"Hi, Mom."

"Hey, hun. Hey, Parker! Come on in."

She holds the door as Eloise and Parker move past her. They walk into the warm kitchen. The house is quiet, except for the TV in the living room.

"Are those peanut butter bars?" Parker spies a covered baking pan sitting on the counter.

"They sure are!" Her mom smiles broadly at Parker and he grins back at her.

Look who's magically in a good mood now.

"Yes!" Parker raises his fist into the air and her mom laughs. Parker's eyes don't match the rest of his face, though her mom doesn't seem to notice. Eloise looks away from them and frowns slightly at the bars instead.

I hate peanut butter desserts.

It stings a little that her mom is so willing to make Parker's favorite foods and never Eloise's. Eloise doesn't understand it. Her mom did the same thing with Eloise's brother-in-law when he still came to family events. She tried talking about it to her mom once and her mom changed the subject, one of her most used strategies to avoid conflict.

What a stupid thing to notice and be upset about. Grow up.

Parker interrupts her sulking by handing her his coat so he can join her dad on the couch to watch the game. She walks down the hallway to the spare bedroom where the coats will sit in a pile on the bed. On her way back to the kitchen, family pictures hanging in the hallway catch her attention. From kindergarten through graduation, she and her sister each have a side of the wall. In between the sisters' frames are a series of family photos taken throughout the years. Stuck into the corner of her sister's wedding picture is a small photo of her nephew as a toddler, the last picture her sister gave to her parents before she cut them all off.

How old is he now? Nine? Ten? I can't believe it's been that long...

Eloise pictures her nephew in her mind, considering what his laugh would be like and what he's interested in as a pre-teen. She can see him so clearly it's as if he's standing beside her, more than half her height. His hair is the same color as her sister's and he has–

Her dad's belly laugh over a joke Parker told interrupts the vision.

What the hell is going on with me tonight? Can pregnancy cause hallucinations?

As she walks back into the kitchen, she makes a mental note to look this up later. Parker stands up to follow behind her, a wide smile on his face. He rubs her back sweetly and then wraps his arm around her shoulders. It's easy to remember what attracted her to him when they're with other people. His sense of humor shines and his affection comes easily.

But he isn't like that at home anymore...

So is this just all for show?

Her mom walks in front of her to take a pan from the oven.

"I like that top, Mom."

"Oh, thanks. I debated wearing it because I think it makes me look fat."

Eloise looks at her petite mother, who weighs the same as she did in high school, and rolls her eyes.

Throughout her entire childhood she must have spent hours sitting on her mom's bed, watching her mom look at herself in the mirror, scrutinizing every perceived flaw- being too fat, a pimple on her face, finding gray hairs, and on and on.

"Mom... you look great."

How many times have I said that to her?

And yet I'd say it a hundred more if it would help her feel better about herself.

Her mom replies sarcastically, "Sure. Okay."

She sees her mom look towards her and can feel her examining her outfit top to bottom. Eloise unconsciously pulls her oversize cardigan tighter to hide more of her body.

"That's an interesting top."

"Interesting," meaning she doesn't like it.

Her mom continues before she can reply.

"Oh– did you hear about the van that caught on fire in the Walmart parking lot?"

Parker laughs abrasively and Eloise flinches slightly at the loudness of it.

"What? How did that happen?" he asks.

Eloise half-listens to her mom share the latest town gossip. She thought of telling her mom she was pregnant tonight but doesn't want to do it within Parker's earshot.

I don't really want to tell her, anyway. Who knows what she'll say?

After dinner, Eloise goes to the bedroom to get their coats. She passes by the pictures on the wall again, her sister's smiling face catching her eye.

I miss her. I wish I hadn't defended Mom and Dad during The Fight.

Eloise pushes those unpleasant memories aside as she returns to the kitchen.

Without thinking it through, she asks her mom a question that has bothered her for the last several years.

Maybe enough time has passed and we can talk about it...

"Hey, Mom. Have you reached out to–"

Uh oh.

She stops talking when she sees the sudden change in her mom's face. "Nevermind," Eloise mutters.

"Who? Your sister?" her mom asks moodily. "Of course not. She told me I was an awful mother."

I don't remember her saying that...

"She cut us out of her life for no good reason. She doesn't care if we're part of it anymore, so why should I contact her?"

Eloise watches her mom walk away huffily, considering if she should follow her to apologize or try to smooth it over somehow.

Sometimes that makes it worse though... I just shouldn't have said anything.

Eloise and Parker wait a few more minutes to see if she'll return. When she doesn't, they wave goodbye to her dad from the doorway. The radio is the only noise in the car on the drive home.

Lucy

Lucy hears Allen answer the front door, followed by her nephew's excited greeting and running footsteps. Miles runs into the kitchen and before Lucy can say anything, his little arms wrap around her legs.

"Hi!"

Lucy bends down to give him a proper hug.

"Hi, Miles! How are you?"

Miles pulls away, and his eyes are wide.

"Good! We had a Valentine's party at school!"

"Fun! Did you get lots of Valentines?"

"Yeah! And I gave one to the girl I like!" Miles giggles and Bree walks in, smiling and shaking her head.

"I'm going to go play with Drew!" Miles runs out of the room as fast as he came into it.

"Oh, boy." Lucy smiles at Bree.

"Yeah... I know."

"Good luck with him as a teenager," Lucy jokes.

"Hey, Luce!" Erik walks in and gives Lucy a bear hug. "Congrats!"

"Thanks." She peeks through his arms at Bree. "I didn't say you could tell him!"

Bree shrugs but looks at Lucy apologetically. "You should know by now that I can't keep secrets."

"I know. I'm just teasing."

Lucy turns around to finish setting the food out for dinner. She puts on

49

her pink quilted oven mitts, ones she took from her grandma's house before the estate sale. She removes the heavy pan from the oven and sets it on top of the stove, then carefully peels off the aluminum foil to reveal the delightfully browned, bubbly top of her "famous" lasagna.

"That smells amazing." Allen comes into the room. "Do you need help with anything, Lucy?"

"Could you get plates and silverware out?"

Allen opens the cupboard and drawer and then sets the plates and utensils on the counter. He also gets out cups and drinks.

"Do you have a bowl I can put the salad in?" Bree asks.

"Yup, there's a big bamboo one in the cupboard." Lucy points with one hand while turning the oven timer off with her other. "Can you get some salad tongs for her, Allen?"

"I brought dessert too. Your favorite."

"Lemon bars?!?"

"Of course! What else?"

"Yum! Thanks! If there are any left, you can leave them here." Lucy winks.

"Already planning on it."

"Dinner's ready!" Lucy calls into the living room.

The sisters get the little ones settled into their booster seats and set their plates in front of them.

"I don't like lasagna!" Miles yells.

"Me either!" Drew copies.

All that work to make it...

"Drew, you ate lasagna last time."

"No!"

"Drew."

"NO!"

Drew's lip juts out, the first sign he's squaring himself for battle. Lucy rolls her neck and closes her eyes. She silently counts to three.

"You know the rule is one bite."

Allen brings his plate to the table.

Trying to reason with Drew, he says, "You like breadsticks and we can get you a cheese stick. Do you want one too, Miles?"

Lucy stares at Allen, speechless.

Unbelievable.

Thanks for undermining my parenting, man.

"What?" he asks her, confusion in his eyes. The others have become intensely focused on their plates, except Drew and Miles who are sticking their tongues out at each other.

"Can you get them cheese sticks while I get my food?" She gestures her head meaningfully toward the kitchen.

"Oh. Yeah." Allen stands up, head slightly lowered.

Once they're alone in the kitchen, she turns to him and whispers, "I was handling it. We can't give him everything he wants all the time."

"I wasn't. I just didn't want to make it a big deal in front of company."

"The research says–"

"Lucy," Allen starts gently, "sometimes the research doesn't help you in the moment."

She turns her back and aggressively puts salad on her plate. A piece of spinach falls onto the floor.

Allen picks it up and tosses it into the garbage. He places his hand lightly on her back while she continues to fill her plate.

"I'm sorry if you felt like I wasn't letting you parent. Maybe we should figure out a sign to use when one of us is handling it and one for when we need the other person to tap in."

Lucy looks up at him, her temper slightly cooler.

"That's a good idea. Let's talk about it later."

Allen kisses her cheek and takes two mozzarella sticks out of the fridge.

Lucy returns to the warmly lit dining room and sees half of Drew's lasagna is gone with another forkful heading to his mouth. She smirks at his sauce-covered face and makes eye contact with Allen across the table. She takes an especially cheesy bite, swallowing her pride with it.

Maybe I don't know everything about parenting just because I have a PhD.

"This lasagna is so good, Aunt Lucy."

"Thanks, Liam. How is school going?"

51

"Good. We got a new kid in class."

"Oh? A boy or girl?"

"Boy. He likes Pokémon too."

"Awesome. Maybe you can be best friends."

The conversation continues to flow easily as they eat. The kids have already left their seats to go play in the living room again when Bree goes to the kitchen to get the lemon bars.

"Lucy gets the first one," she says when she returns.

"Yes!"

Allen leans back, wipes powdered sugar from his lips, and rubs his stomach contentedly.

"You two cooked, so we'll clean up right, Erik?"

"Oh, sure." Erik fake sighs dramatically and his hand lightly grazes Bree's back as he walks by.

Bree stands up and pokes her head into the living room, momentarily quieting the happy chaos that's been occurring.

"It's almost time to go. Choose one more thing to do, kids." She turns to Lucy. "Your *Monstera* is getting so big!"

"I can propagate some for you."

"That'd be great! Erik left the snake plant you gave me outside this fall, and it died."

Lucy gasps and whispers, "That's divorce-able."

"I heard that," Erik yells from the kitchen.

Bree laughs as she covers the lemon bars back up.

"Hey, wait," Lucy says. "Give me another one of those. The baby wants one more."

Eloise

Eloise is sitting on a park bench, her legs loosely crossed at the ankles. She's watching a little girl play happily on the playground. Giant trees cast shadows on the green grass of the park. She looks up and sees the branches wave across the blue sky in a gentle, warm breeze, noting that it's much warmer here than at home. As she watches, a blackbird flies from one branch to another. It hops a few times, then flies to another tree on the other side of the playground. Eloise continues to watch the little girl as she runs across the wood chips. The bird flies to the tree closest to Eloise. It hops down from the branch and lands on the bench next to her. Eloise looks at it as it gazes back at her.

"Can I help you with something?"

The bird turns its head slightly but remains silent.

"Great, now I'm talking to a bird..."

Eloise wakes up with a start, snapping her eyes open.

Super, this pregnancy is causing weird dreams now too.

Parker is still sleeping deeply beside her. She leaves the bedroom quietly, so she doesn't wake him.

Wish he could be as thoughtful...

She woke up when he finally came to bed hours after her, smelling like a greasy dive bar. The smell made her so nauseous she almost had to leave the bedroom.

Eloise turns on the kitchen light, surprised to see that the automatic coffee pot has just started brewing.

Oh, he remembered to fill it last night.

53

Now I feel guilty that I just complained about him.

She takes two of her favorite mugs from the cupboard, vintage souvenir mugs she snagged at a garage sale for $1 each. One has a sketch of Niagara Falls (hers) and the other features a bear and advertises Yosemite National Park (Parker's, *for obvious reasons most days*).

She moves automatically about the room, placing a bagel in the toaster, taking the creamer out of the fridge and setting it on the counter. While she waits for her breakfast to finish, she goes to the living room to open the curtains. The sky is just brightening, and she can hear the early morning songs of the birds who have returned from their southern vacations.

As Eloise turns back to the kitchen to pour her coffee, she glimpses a blackbird fly past the window.

What. The. Hell.

Lucy

Lucy stands in their walk-in closet, getting ready for a day of seeing clients at her practice. She rifles through her clothes, looking for something that will fit. She finally pulls on a pair of pants, only to realize they won't zip.

"Dammit," she mutters, before sighing and taking them off.

She wore these pants well into the second trimester with Drew. Unbelievable that they don't fit now, and she's only a couple months along.

Lucy turns to the side in the mirror and looks at the small bulge of her belly. She grabs a looser pair of pants instead, a size bigger than her normal one. She reminds herself that it's just a number and that her body is doing exactly what it's meant to right now.

And even if I wasn't pregnant, who cares about the number?

She turns back so that she's facing the mirror and her eyes drift to her hips and thighs.

But maybe only eat one leftover lemon bar today.

Lucy looks up to her face and startles when she sees her mother staring back.

Allen comes into the room behind her, pulling her eyes away from the mirror. She looks back and sees her own face, but the unsettled feeling lingers.

"You look great." He kisses her cheek and then heads into the bathroom.

Drew calls for her in his bedroom and she walks to get him, taking deep calming breaths all the way down the hall.

"Good morning, buddy. How did you sleep?"

Drew throws his small, warm arms around her and gives her a tight squeeze.

She smiles affectionately against his neck.

"Good." He pulls away and looks at her with wide eyes. "Hey mom, it dark in here."

"Yeah, it is kind of dark."

"Pretty fooky."

Her weird little three-year-old is obsessed with "fooky" things. He's requested they read Halloween books every night for months now.

"It is a little spooky. Let's open the curtain."

She opens it to let in the morning sun. The days are slowly, but finally, getting longer.

"Are you hungry, buddy?"

"Yeah. I want breakfast!"

Lucy picks Drew up and carries him into the kitchen. She pours some milk into a cup and takes out the fruit she cut up for him yesterday.

"Here's some milk and apples. Do you want a granola bar or Cheerios?"

"Cheer-o's!"

She brings the box and a bowl over to the table.

"I want do it!"

"Okay, but let me help you."

"No! I do myself!"

"Okay… Please be careful…"

Her son takes the box from her and within half a second cereal spreads across the entire kitchen table.

"Uh oh." He looks up at her quickly, eyes wide, gauging her reaction.

She closes her eyes and takes a deep breath. And another.

It's too early for this BS.

"I need help," Drew says.

Lucy exhales. "Okay, thank you for asking for help."

Drew grabs the box and together they pour a little into the bowl. She scoops up the pieces from the table and adds them to the rest. Then she bends down to pick up the circles off the floor before they can get crunched into powder, causing an even larger mess.

That's the last thing I need this morning.

Her husband strolls into the room as she's closing the garbage lid.

"Where the heck have you been this whole time?"

"Going to the bathroom. Why?"

Lucy gestures to the remaining pieces on the floor.

"Can you finish cleaning up this cereal? I'm feeling a little sick and would like to eat some toast."

"Sure, hun."

Lucy puts some bread in the toaster as her nausea increases. She takes a drink of water.

"What time is your last class today?"

Before she can answer Allen, she rushes to the bathroom.

Eloise

March

The morning is cold and sunny, perfect for sitting indoors with a warm cup of coffee. Less perfect for having forced conversation with your mother while drinking it.

She knows she's delayed this long enough, though. They were supposed to meet last week, but it was raining and her mom canceled because she didn't want to drive to Eloise's house.

Strange she said that after I told her I had something I wanted to talk about. Like she was avoiding me.

But at least it bought me some extra time.

Her mom arrived a few minutes ago and they've already exhausted the usual chit chat. Now they sit at Eloise's dining table, sipping their coffee silently.

Ever a busybody and neat-freak, Eloise watches her mom stand up to throw a tiny scrap of paper away, then watches her head to the closet to get the broom so she can sweep.

"Mom, you don't have to do that. I can sweep my floor."

"Oh, that's okay. I don't mind helping you if you need it."

Eloise watches her mom sweep and takes a deep breath.

Now or never. Just do it.

She repositions herself in her seat again before clearing her throat. "So... I'm pregnant..."

The broom stops midair as her mom looks up at her.

Is she...disappointed...? Happy? Angry....?

"You are? That's so exciting!"

Eloise feels a weight lift off of her chest.

We're going with excited. Good. Much better than judgmental.

There's an awkward moment when Eloise wonders if her mom will hug her, or if she wants her to.

Instead, her mom goes back to sweeping, smiling this time.

"When are you due?"

"October."

Swish. Swish. Swish.

Her mom finally finishes the floor, sweeps up the tiny pile of dirt, and empties it into the garbage. She returns to her seat and sips the last of her coffee.

"I can't wait for a grandbaby. You were such an easy kid. You never gave us any trouble growing up."

I was easy because I was always too scared to share my opinion or problems. And I never wanted to add more stress to our war zone of a house.

Eloise plays with a string on her sweater sleeve.

Not that she would have listened to me then anyway...

Her mom laughs. "Your sister on the other hand... If I'd had her first, we wouldn't have had a second baby."

As soon as her mom finishes this sentence, her eyes flash a panicked look, and she immediately changes the subject. "Are you and Parker planning on getting married?"

Eloise hasn't even considered it, and he certainly hasn't asked.

There was a time when I wanted to marry him...

"We haven't talked about it."

Her mom shakes her head. "Times are different now, I guess. Is Parker excited?"

"Um.... no. We haven't really talked about it since I told him."

"He'll come around. It's a baby. As soon as he sees his child, he'll fall in love. How could he not?"

Sure hope she's right...

"Do you want more coffee, Mom?"

"That'd be great. Thanks!"

Her mom smiles at her as she extends her mug, oblivious that Eloise clearly doesn't share the same optimism.

Lucy

Ring ring. Pause. Ring–

"Hey!" She hears her neighbor's bright voice in her ear.

"Hey, Emily! Drew and I were about to go for a walk to the library. Do you guys want to join us?"

"Absolutely! Give me ten minutes to finish cleaning up and get the kids dressed."

"Sounds good. Why don't you just come over here when you're ready?"

"Perfect. See you soon!"

Lucy looks at the clock on the living room wall and starts packing the diaper bag. Knowing that children have zero respect for time or plans, she figures she has more than enough time to finish getting ready.

Sure enough, the doorbell rings twenty minutes later while she and Drew are finishing an episode of *The Wiggles*.

She opens the door and before she can say hello Emily asks quickly, "Hey! Can Nora use your bathroom? Apparently, she decided she had to go after all, even though I asked her at home."

"Must have been the walk." Lucy laughs as her gaze drifts to the house number by Emily's door across the lawn.

Emily scoots past her down the hall, a tighter fit than normal with six-month-old Wesley wrapped in a carrier on her chest.

"Drew, Nora is here, so we can go to the library."

"The library!?!" He bounces off the couch and runs to the door.

"Fruit salad, yumm–" Lucy turns off the TV, ending the song.

Enough of that, but God bless them for providing kids with some wholesome entertainment.

"Let's get your shoes on." Lucy heads to the entryway to take Drew's shoes out of the basket.

Fruit salad.... Shit. Now it's stuck in my head.

Emily and Nora come out of the bathroom. "Alright. Now I think we're ready."

Lucy finishes helping Drew with his shoes, and they finally head out the door.

Drew and Nora run ahead of them.

"Not too far, you two!" Emily calls out to them. It's a chilly but sunny day. The trees are still bare of leaves and a few birds perch at the tops, calling out to one another with their mid-morning songs. The street is quiet except for their calls and the occasional car passing by. Emily and Lucy hurry to stay close to their energetic firstborns. Wesley bounces up and down with Emily's quick steps.

"Do you like that wrap?"

"I love it! I use it all the time so that I can still do things around the house and play with Nora."

Lucy nods, debating how much she wants to say next.

"I never used one with Drew, but I'll probably need one for Baby Number Two."

Emily turns her head, eyes wide, but hesitant to ask what Lucy knows she's thinking. "Are you...?"

Lucy smiles, shyly, but happily, while responding. "Yes."

"Ohhh! Lucy! I'm so excited!"

"We aren't telling most people yet. It's still early."

"I won't say a word. Obviously, Jon doesn't count, unless you don't want me telling him."

"You can tell him. Allen may tell him too, or knowing him, he probably already did."

"And then Jon forgot to tell me. Typical." She shakes her head and sighs dramatically.

"Stop at the tree, Drew!" Lucy yells out.

He keeps going.

"Stop!"

She jogs quickly to catch up to him, and just inches past the tree, grabs his arm.

Drew looks up at her with wide, surprised eyes, and she realizes he never heard her call out.

"Sorry, hun. I didn't want you to walk into the road. I just wanted to keep you safe."

They all cross the empty street and walk under the library's awning. Lucy stops before opening the door and looks at the two toddlers seriously.

"Remember, we need to be quiet in here."

"Okay!" Drew whispers, and Nora nods solemnly.

Lucy lets them inside and whisper-yells "Walk!" as they race under her arm. They slow their steps in response as they bend to go through the tiny doorway cut into a giant fake tree, the magical gateway to the children's area.

The adults use the door next to it. Lucy secretly wishes she could experience the same magic her son does as she enters one of her favorite places. Libraries and books have always been her favorite way to escape reality.

I love to disassociate on a page.

Nerd.

Emily takes Wesley out of the carrier and sets him on the floor with some baby toys. Lucy gets the wooden blocks off the shelf for Nora and Drew.

Emily quietly asks her, "How have you been feeling?"

"Sick."

"That's the worst."

"Yeah. It's made it hard to get stuff done between work and home. Looking forward to that part ending so maybe I can feel less behind all the time."

She watches Drew and Nora stacking blocks before turning back to Emily.

"How have you been? Anything new?"

"Not really. I think I'm going back to work part time now that this one is a little older." She hands Wesley a rattle ball, which he shakes enthusiastically.

"At the same company?"

"Probably not. They wouldn't let me work from home. Medical billing isn't exactly glamorous, so if I can do it from the comfort of my dining room and stay home with this guy, I'm going to."

"That probably would make breastfeeding easier, too."

"Absolutely. I'll do anything to avoid pumping this time around."

I still need to buy a new pump.

Dread fills her stomach as she remembers counting every precious ounce, constantly worried she wouldn't have enough for baby Drew.

Maybe it'll be easier this time.

A loud crash followed by an even louder cry rings out in the quiet room. Wooden blocks clutter the floor.

Nora sits among them, distraught.

"What's wrong, honey?" Emily asks her.

"Drew push tower!"

Drew has moved behind a shelf. His eyes are wide as he peers between books at his mom.

"Drew. Come here," Lucy says in a quiet Mom voice.

"No."

"Drew."

"NO!"

Recognizing she won't win this battle and wanting to avoid a scene, Lucy walks over to Drew. He looks down at the floor.

"Drew, it isn't nice to hurt other people's things. Nora is sad now. See? She's crying." Lucy points at his little friend, who is sniffling against her mom's shoulders.

"Let's go say we're sorry." She takes his hand and pulls him lightly back to the blocks. "What do you need to say to Nora to help her feel better?"

Drew continues staring at the floor but glances up through his heavy lashes. "Sorry," he mumbles.

"Thank you, Drew," Emily says. "Can you say thank you to Drew, Nora?"

"No!"

Lucy shakes her head slightly at Emily, letting her know it's okay.

"Let's get something else out for you, Drew. How about the train track?"

Lucy and Emily get both children settled back into playing and return to their seats.

Lucy smiles tiredly at her friend. "None of the baby books prepared me for parenting a toddler."

"Me either. And just think, we get to do it again." Emily looks down at Wesley, shaking his rattle ball like a maraca. "Do you think parenting was easier before the internet existed as a constant comparison to other parents? I'm confident my parents never even read a parenting book."

Lucy laughs sarcastically. "Oh, mine definitely didn't either." She watches Drew pushing his train and sees his lips whispering a story as it passes through tunnels and over wooden mountains. Tenderness softens her tone as she says, "Maybe our second kids will make us experts, and we can write a book."

"Yeah, we'll call it *No Parent Knows What They're Doing. We're All Just Doing Our F-ing Best.*"

"With the tag of *And hope you like getting back up right after you sit down,*" Lucy adds. "Why doesn't anyone tell you how little you'll sit as a parent?"

"Seriously, lady. We may be onto something with this book idea."

"Move over, Super Nanny," Lucy says dryly.

Nora walks over to Drew and asks him if she can play. Lucy watches as Drew hands her a train so they can race them around the track.

"Chugga chugga choo choo!"

She smiles at their delighted giggles.

You aren't doing so bad though, Mama.

Eloise

Eloise and Sarah are having lunch in the conference room again. The smell of their boss's microwaved cod in the break room made Eloise gag five feet from the doorway.

Only a sociopath warms up fish in a SHARED microwave.

"What have you been watching lately?" Sarah asks her before taking a bite of her salad. Eloise notices Sarah switched from vinaigrette dressing to ranch and can't help but wonder if she did that for her. She doesn't want to ask, but it would be like Sarah to notice all on her own.

"Nothing really. Most nights Parker has some game or show on. Sometimes when he isn't home I'll put on *The Office*."

"I love that show. It's one of my comfort shows."

"Mine too." Eloise doesn't add that it's been on a lot lately. She's been home alone more nights than normal since they found out she was pregnant. When he is home, they're lucky to say three sentences to each other. Even luckier when at least one is something positive.

He did the dishes last night, which was sweet and unexpected though. Oh, and he brought me that coffee last Saturday after he'd been out!

It's not all bad then.

"What about you? What have you been watching?" Eloise asks.

"We started watching the new series about Ted Bundy. It's great, sucks you right in."

"Interesting. I don't like scary shows or movies."

"It isn't really scary, but it's interesting in a sick and twisted kind of way. You should check it out."

"I've been pretty tired lately, so I haven't wanted to start anything new. Most nights, I end up falling asleep on the couch." Eloise picks at her food, taking small bites here and there.

"How have you been feeling? Just tired?" Sarah asks, a note of empathy touching her voice.

"Yeah, I've been a little nauseous, especially after I take my vitamins." Eloise takes a bite of cracker before continuing. "I told my mom I was pregnant."

"Oh yeah? Is she excited?"

"Yeah, she is."

Sarah looks at her intently before looking back down at her lunch. She moves some salad around with her fork. Eloise hasn't told her much about her family and Sarah isn't always one to pry.

Just sometimes.

"How did Parker take the news? I forgot to ask."

"Not well. We haven't talked about it since..." Her foot taps on the ground lightly and she sees Sarah look down towards it. Eloise stills it.

Please don't say or ask anything else. I don't want to talk about it.

Sarah seems to sense her discomfort and changes the subject.

"If you aren't busy, I'm going to a yoga class next week and could use some company. It's a beginner class, so you won't feel out of place, and I assume it would be fine, given your current condition."

"Oh, okay. I'll think about it. I should talk to Parker and see if we have plans."

Her vision becomes wavy, and Eloise suddenly sees lifelike images flash into her mind.

Holding hands with a man.

A toddler on her lap with the man's arm around her shoulders.

Him gently kissing her temple...

Eloise blinks quickly and sees Sarah looking closely at her, eyes narrowed.

"Are you okay?" Eloise can hear the concern in her friend's voice.

"Yes, why?"

"You had a weird look on your face."

"Just daydreaming." Eloise smiles tiredly before taking another small bite of food. "I told you I've been tired."

And maybe losing my mind...

If it happens again, I'll call the doctor's office....

They finish their lunch, and the thought that's been on Eloise's mind follows her back to her desk.

Who were those people?

Lucy

Lucy cleans up dinner in the kitchen while her father-in-law, Tim, plays with Drew in the living room. Allen's parents are visiting from out of state.

"Ready for another space flight?" Tim asks Drew.

"Yay!"

Lucy smiles, bitterness and guilt painting the edges of it, as she listens to Drew giggling.

It's unfair that his other grandparents have abandoned him.

But I'm partially to blame for that too.

Should I–?

Her mother-in-law interrupts her thoughts.

"How has work been, Lucy?" Joan asks.

"Good. My schedule is more flexible this semester, which has been really nice for spending extra time with Drew."

"That's great. I know everyone says it, but it goes fast, doesn't it?"

"3-2-1.... Blast off! Shoooooo!" Tim shouts.

Lucy nods and watches as Tim flies Drew past the doorway. Joan continues.

"I was thinking- if you and Allen want to get away for a night while we're here, we can stay with Drew."

"Oh." Lucy keeps her voice monotone, but internally panics. "That's nice of you to offer."

Would Drew be okay staying alone with them?

We've never left him with anyone overnight. What if he needs us?

What if something happens and I'm not here?

"I'll think about it. It might be hard to find a hotel room at the last minute.

Maybe we can sneak away for a couple of hours, though."

Lucy turns away from Joan and her tight ponytail swishes over her shoulder. She calls into the living room, "Okay, time to settle down. Bedtime is coming soon."

She hears Allen get up from the couch.

"Party's over, guys. Let's get you ready for your bath, Drew."

Tim flies Drew into the bathroom while Allen runs water for the tub. Toy boats float on top and bubbles pile under the faucet.

"Bubbles!"

After he's clean and the water has turned chilly, Lucy wraps Drew snugly in a towel. She hugs him tightly, dries him off, and dresses him in his favorite dinosaur pajamas. Joan peeks in as she walks down the hallway.

"Do you want Grandma to take you to bed tonight?" Lucy asks him.

Bedtime is my favorite moment of the day, but I can share tonight.

That would give me a chance to catch up on some stuff.

"Yeah! Can we read *Goodnight Moon*, please?"

"Of course. I read that to your daddy when he was your age."

Lucy kisses Drew's forehead and tells him goodnight. He jogs from the room and Joan follows with a nostalgic smile on her face.

Allen heads to the kitchen to do the dishes while Lucy folds laundry in the bedroom.

Who would have guessed that in your thirties you'd look forward to your relatives providing you with respite so you could catch up on chores?

Allen and Lucy eventually join Tim in the living room to sit around the fireplace. After Drew finally falls asleep, Joan stealthily sneaks out of his room. Lucy asks if they'd like to open a bottle of wine. They agree and she goes to the kitchen, bringing back only three wine glasses.

She sees her mother-in-law clock this, but Joan, tactfully, doesn't comment.

Lucy and Allen make eye contact. She raises her brows meaningfully at him.

"So, we have some news…" Allen starts.

"I knew it!" Joan exclaims.

"Knew what?" Tim asks, confused.

Lucy and Allen laugh.

"Lucy's pregnant," Allen says.

"Oh, you guys! That's great!" Tim's voice cracks with emotion and his eyes get misty. "When are you due, Lucy?" Joan asks.

"October."

"Man, we were going to ask if you wanted to come visit us this fall, but looks like we'll be coming here instead, huh, Joanie?"

"If that's okay," Joan quickly adds as she glances sternly at her husband.

"Of course it's okay. We love it when you visit."

Lucy is careful to use the word "visit." She loves their short, temporary company. She knows her mother-in-law would move in for an extended stay, and while she wouldn't say no to the extra help, the introvert in her cannot handle long-term company.

"Please let us know how we can help, okay? We don't want to be a burden, but we'd love to make things easier for you."

Allen replies for both of them, "We will. Thanks, guys."

Lucy and Allen snuggle on the sofa, covered by a knitted blanket. Joan and Tim sit on the loveseat across from them. Joan's feet rest comfortably on Tim's legs. Lucy feels content and thinks about how she won the lottery for in-laws.

My parents would never sit like that.

The living room shimmers, and her mind suddenly fills with a different picture. She's sitting alone in a dimly lit, slightly shabby room. The TV is on, and her head rests on her hand as she stares at the screen mindlessly.

Drew's cry interrupts the vision.

"I'll go get him." She stands up quickly. Allen hears the strangeness in her tone and looks at her closely. She smiles at him, hoping it seems reassuring.

If it happens one more time, I'll tell Dr. Hadley they're back.

Eloise

Eloise sits by herself in the cramped, outdated waiting room of her OB's office. She didn't bother asking Parker to come. The fluorescent lights flicker above her and there's a plant beside her that looks like it needs watering.

A nurse with major RBF opens the door, looks down at her clipboard and in monotone calls out, "Eloise."

Eloise gets up from her chair and walks through the doorway into a hall of faded linoleum.

"How's your day going today?" Major RBF asks her flatly.

"Fine."

The nurse completes all the preliminary measurements and tests before leaving Eloise alone to wait for the doctor. Today will be the first time she meets him. Until now, her appointments have been with just nurses. She waits only a few minutes before a quick knock sounds on the door.

A man who must be nearing retirement enters the room and introduces himself as Dr. Sattler. Eloise is fairly sure that this is the same doctor who delivered her sister over twenty-five years ago.

Just not gonna think about that too much.

The doctor shakes her hand before sitting on his rolling stool. He asks her how she's feeling.

"Fine. Tired, just a little nauseous."

"That's typical. No bleeding or cramping?"

"No."

Should I tell him I might be losing my mind?

Before she can decide, he's asking her more questions about prenatal vitamins and if she smokes. Satisfied with her brief answers, he pushes on with the appointment.

"At this point in pregnancy, we offer a screening test to moms to check for genetic disorders. It's optional, but we recommend it to provide you with the best care."

"Um…" Eloise pauses, unsure. She shifts her body on the exam table, crinkling the paper. Would she want to know the results if something was wrong? Would it change anything for her or just make this difficult situation even harder?

"Can I think about it?" she asks.

"Absolutely. We have to do it before twenty-two weeks, so just call us before your next appointment so we can send the lab work in for you. It's just a simple blood test."

"Okay. Thanks."

"No problem. Do you have any questions about it?"

"No, I don't think so."

"Well, let us know if you do." Dr. Sattler stands up and gets his materials ready. "Okay, let's see if we can hear a heartbeat. It might be a little soon, but sometimes we can hear it at this point."

He has Eloise lay back on the table and lifts her shirt slightly to expose her abdomen.

"This will be a little cold."

He squeezes a cool, jellylike substance onto Eloise's stomach and pushes a probe gently against her skin. He moves it around a few times, and all Eloise hears is a muffled whooshing noise. She shifts her legs slightly, trying to get comfortable. Dr. Sattler finally settles the probe in one place and adjusts the device.

Then she hears it.

A clipping, galloping noise.

"There it is."

Eloise looks up at the speckled ceiling tiles and listens. Her eyes sting, her throat feels tight, and she stifles a sob. Dr. Sattler glances at her and smiles.

"Amazing isn't it?"

Yes, but I wish I wasn't here alone...

Eloise nods and wipes a stray tear from her eye. After several more seconds, the doctor removes the device and hands her a paper towel to wipe the jelly off her stomach.

"Anything else for me today?"

Eloise shakes her head.

"Okay, let us know if anything comes up and what you decide about the Quad test. I'll see you at your next appointment."

Eloise wipes the remaining tears from her eyes as her doctor shuts the door on his way out. She collects her things and leaves the room to drive herself home.

* * *

Later she selects "Mom" from her contact list. The Quad test hasn't left her mind.

Was it even offered when my mom was pregnant?

"Hello?" her mom answers on the first ring.

"Hi, what are you up to?"

"Working on my grocery list for the week."

"Fun. I had a question for you..."

"Okay." Her mom waits quietly. Eloise can hear her pen scratching on a notepad on the other end.

"Um. I had a doctor's appointment today, and he asked if I wanted to have genetic screening done."

More pen scratching, but otherwise, silence.

"And... I don't know what to think about it. I was hoping you could help me decide."

"Well, I never had it done and you both turned out fine."

"Right..."

"I guess you'll have to think about it," her mom says, half-distracted.

Super glad I called for that goldmine of wisdom.

"Do you–"

74

Her mom interrupts her, leaving Eloise's question unfinished.

"How was your appointment?"

"Fine. I heard the heartbeat."

"Oh! That's so sweet!"

"Yeah. It was. Do you want to come with me to an appointment sometime? It might be nice to have some company…"

"Maybe. If you have any on Tuesdays I might be able to come." Eloise hears her mom shuffling things around. "Alright, I'm about done with this list and then I need to put my makeup on so we can go to town."

Eloise murmurs goodbye and hangs up, just as lost as she was ten minutes ago.

Lucy

Lucy rests on the couch snuggled up in a Sherpa blanket with Drew. Two piles of children's books, one read and another to-read, sit on the coffee table in front of them. Plants overflow from the corners and shelves, and a beeswax candle glows brightly on the mantle. A late spring snow falls slowly outside the windows.

The doorbell interrupts their quiet moment.

"I get it!" Drew tumbles off the couch and runs to the front door.

"Let me help, buddy."

As they open the door, cool fresh air enters the room. Their neighbors stand on the porch, arriving for their scheduled play date.

"Nora!" Drew jumps and shouts.

"Come on in, guys."

Lucy holds the door for them and then closes it once they step inside. A toy drops from the diaper bag and Lucy discreetly picks it up and tucks it back in without Emily even noticing. She takes Wesley so that Emily can help Nora take her shoes off. Lucy smiles at him and makes funny faces, the type reserved specially for those under the age of three.

She looks down at the other children while saying, "Drew has his toys set up in the living room if you want to go play with him, Nora."

Nora and Drew race through the hall and slide into the living room. Lucy hands Wesley back to his mom.

"Thanks for having us. Nora has been asking for another playdate."

"No problem. I'm glad it worked out. Do you want some coffee?"

"Absolutely, if you don't mind. This guy has been disrupting my beauty rest." Emily looks away from Lucy to tickle Wesley under the chin and he giggles with a throaty belly laugh.

"I'm not looking forward to doing that again. The newborn stage is my least favorite and I'm already dreading the lack of sleep."

"Has your morning sickness gotten better?"

"I think so. Finally."

Emily and Lucy set their matching cream speckled mugs on the dining room table where they can still see into the living room and watch the children play. Emily perches Wesley on her lap at first, but when he wiggles to get down, she lays him on the shag rug with his toys. She takes a sip from her steaming mug and then closes her eyes.

"Mmm. You make the best coffee, Lucy."

Lucy smiles, stupidly proud of her coffee brewing skills. "Thanks."

"Where's Allen?"

"At a work conference for the last few days. He'll be home later today, though."

"Oh, I didn't realize he was away. How was your time without him?"

"It was kind of hard managing everything alone, but we survived."

"I could have helped you. You should have asked."

"You just told me you aren't sleeping well!" Lucy exclaims, a hint of laughter in her voice. "It's okay. I've gotten pretty good at managing on my own when I need to."

Unfortunately.

Lucy takes a sip of her warm coffee before continuing.

"Joan and Tim were actually here over the weekend. I thought about asking them to stay a little longer, but they've had their flights booked for months. I didn't want to make them change their plans."

They drink their coffee and watch the toddlers play peacefully.

"How was your time with Allen's parents?" Emily asks.

"It was nice. They watched Drew so Allen and I could go out alone for a few hours, which was good for us."

And Drew was fine.

And so were you.

Lucy blows lightly into her mug. "It's nice they actually like being here and part of our lives, unlike my parents."

Shoot, didn't mean to open that door...

"Sorry, that sounded way more bitter than I intended," Lucy tries to correct herself, hoping Emily lets it go.

What else can I talk about?

Ugh, why is my mind totally blank?

Oh! Talk about the restaurant you ate at.

Emily's lips start to move.

Too late.

"I know you don't talk to your parents, but you've never told me why. You don't have to tell me if you don't want to."

There it is.

Lucy sighs. "No. It's fine. I can share a little."

"Talking about hard things helps." Just like Dr. Hadley says.

Her foot hits the table rhythmically several times, causing some of her coffee to splash lightly against the rim of the ceramic mug. She looks toward the window and watches large white snowflakes drop lightly to the ground.

Where to start though...

A heaviness settles in her chest, and she takes a breath to unblock it as memories flood her mind, one after another.

Her dad yelling, while her mom says nothing.

Lucy hiding under her sheets, her head covered and her hands over her ears.

Her mom coming into her bedroom later, sitting down on her bed, and crying.

Talking to her like she's an adult girlfriend rather than her young daughter, telling her things she's too little to understand.

"My parents had a really difficult marriage. I think they each came to it with their own baggage but never wanted to admit it."

She uncrosses her legs and then recrosses them before finally sitting still.

"We don't have to talk about this if you don't want to, Luce."

"No, it really is okay, and my therapist would be clapping for me," Lucy says. "It created a lot of problems for them and a pretty unhappy childhood for me and my sister. I never felt comfortable at home and when I look back, the memories that are the clearest aren't happy ones."

Empty beer cans all over the living room.

Her mom picking them up angrily while her dad snores heavily on the couch.

Complaining about him to her and her sister.

Seeing the bruise on her mom's arm as she lifts a can from the floor.

Emily's eyes soften. "I'm sorry, Lucy."

Lucy backtracks a little, as she always does when confronted with others' sympathy. "Obviously we had nice moments, too."

None come to mind right now...

But there must have been some.

"There were also a lot of things I normalized then, things that were actually messed up. Like, I went through some s-h-i-t and didn't even know it."

Lucy laughs and Emily joins in.

"My sister and I weren't hit or anything, thankfully. For the longest time, I hated to compare my home to ones where even worse things happened. Eventually though, I realized I had to admit that my childhood wasn't normal and that it had a big impact on me."

Feeling the constant pressure to always "fix" things.

Or at least to not make things worse.

My perfectionistic tendencies.

All the failed relationships before Allen.

Drew's scared face when I lose my temper...

Lucy blinks the last image away, along with a couple of tears. She shifts her weight in the cushioned dining chair slightly so that she's sitting more comfortably. "I finally decided that I had to stop letting those bad childhood memories and feelings control me. When I did, the relationship with my parents seemed to end."

"What was it that made you officially decide to break off contact with them?" Emily asks quietly over her coffee mug.

"I don't know that I decided, not intentionally, anyway. But I realized I was constantly reliving all my worst childhood memories and feelings with nearly every interaction. I was so unhappy all the time and finally saw how unhealthy my relationship with them was, with the help of my therapist of course." Lucy chuckles without humor.

Like when my mom skipped my wedding dress appointment for some half-ass reason I can't remember now.

Or my dad calling for bail money.

Multiple times.

As she's transported back to these memories, she feels the hurt and disappointment just as deeply as she first did.

"The tipping point was when I found out I was pregnant with Drew, I decided it wasn't fair to him either. I couldn't have my own kids experience what I did. They deserve the best mom I can be."

"That's a sweet goal. What happened after you knew you were pregnant?"

Her stomach churns as she hears muffled lines from those hard conversations.

"I tried talking to them. That didn't go well."

Her mom's (*fake?*) tears.

Lucy pulls the sleeves of her chenille sweater down so she can feel the softness of it against her palms. She spins the beaded bracelet on her wrist.

"My mom gave me the usual lines like, 'I'm sorry I'm such a terrible mother.' I never said those words to her and don't even think that. And my dad..."

Her dad's hurt face, before he started yelling at her.

"That conversation was worse." Lucy takes another deep breath before continuing. She tightens her hair tie, pulling her sleek ponytail higher.

"Neither was willing to really listen. I tried a couple more times, but it felt like I was investing so much energy into relationships where I just kept getting hurt. I finally couldn't do it anymore and had to set a boundary with them to protect myself. It still feels really unfair that I was in that position."

"When was the last time you've seen or talked to them?" Emily asks.

"Over three years. It was really hard, and it still is honestly. I don't even know where they live now. They divorced several ago, before I stopped talking to them. We tried to still get together with them, separately of course.

They can't be in the same room without making everyone in it uncomfortable. I think people have made up reasons to leave rooms they're in together. How many times do you hear people say their basements flooded and that they need to leave? I've heard it at least twice." Lucy and Emily's chuckles break the somber mood in the room.

"Mama! Help me!"

Drew brings his superhero cape over and hands it to Lucy. She fastens it around his neck.

"Thanks, Mama!" Lucy and Emily both smile as they watch him run back into the cozy living room with his fists raised in front of his little torso.

Lucy's eyes fill with tears, and her voice thickens with emotion.

"Do you know what the hardest part is? They just let it happen, just walked away from their own kids."

Emily's eyes look misty as well. "I'm sorry, Lucy. I'm so close to my mom that I can't imagine not having a relationship with her."

"I know, and as a mother myself now, I'll never understand it. I can't imagine not having Drew in my life." She feels a little breathless and her voice cracks slightly as she says, "I feel like an orphan, and it kills me that my kids won't know their grandparents. My parents don't even know about Drew or this baby coming I don't think. I certainly haven't told them."

"That sucks, Lucy, and I'm so sorry. I don't really know what else to say." Emily pauses as she considers her next words. "It sounds like you tried, though."

"I know, but it didn't change the result. We haven't even talked about the guilt I feel for not talking to my own parents, for not trying harder. Even if no one says it aloud when they find out, I'm always left feeling judged, like I'm the villain."

"You don't talk to your parents?"

"Can't you just forgive them?"

"Your own mom and dad?"

Lucy sips her coffee, a giant weight of loneliness hanging over her despite sharing all of this with Emily. She stares into her mug and says, "And I feel like I'm parenting without a village, which sucks honestly." Lucy smiles sadly as she wipes her eyes. "I'm slowly creating a village, but it isn't the same as having the people who raised you at the center."

"I'll be part of your village, lady. And for what it's worth, I don't think you're a villain. If you were, you'd be a smoking hot one, though."

Lucy chuckles and rubs her growing stomach. "Especially in my current state." Emily laughs and Lucy smiles again, feeling some of the heaviness finally lift.

She sets her coffee mug back down and watches the liquid swirl. A vision of her mom walking away angrily springs into her mind. She can't tell if it's a memory or something else, but before she can decide, it's gone as quickly as it came. The coffee rests peacefully in her mug.

Eloise

Eloise is sitting on the couch, a colorful striped afghan her great-grandma made tucked around her. She's scrolling through the baby app on her phone when she hears the door open. Parker comes in with a pizza box and a two-liter. He sees her and smiles warmly. Eloise hides her surprise as she meets his gaze.

What's going on...?

"I picked up dinner."

"Oh, thanks. That was thoughtful of you." She smiles back hesitantly.

"You're welcome. I thought maybe we could watch a movie tonight."

"I'd like that. What do you want to watch?"

"Why don't you pick?"

"I'd like to see that new rom-com with that actress I like. The one I can never remember her name. Emma Something." Parker rolls his eyes dramatically. Eloise laughs, mostly to humor him. She doesn't want to waste this olive branch he's extending. "But we don't have to. How about an Avengers movie I haven't seen yet?"

"Yeah? Sure!"

Parker sets the box and bottle on the coffee table and gets the movie ready. Eloise goes to the kitchen to get plates and cups.

"How was your day?" she asks.

"Good."

He seems like he's in a good mood, so she tests the waters.

"I had a doctor's appointment today."

83

"Oh, yeah?"

"Yeah. I heard the heartbeat for the first time."

"Neat."

He doesn't seem disappointed he wasn't there, and he doesn't ask when the next appointment is. He also doesn't seem annoyed for once, though.

Maybe this is progress.

She thinks about bringing up the testing the doctor offered but doesn't want to push her luck.

He doesn't ask more about the baby and they eat their pizza and watch the movie in what has become their normal silence. She eventually falls asleep with her head resting on the arm of the couch. It isn't long before her eyes shift back and forth under her closed eyelids.

The blackbird is back, but this time Eloise watches it from a window. It flies back and forth, bringing sticks to build a nest. Parker's muffled voice calls her from somewhere deep inside the house. She turns away from the window to find him.

She wakes up abruptly to Parker kissing her. "The movie's over. You fell asleep," he whispers. "Why don't we go to bed?"

She kisses him back, hoping that this is a chance for them to reconnect and move forward.

II

Trimester Two

Lucy

April

Lucy stands in her university office doorway, trying to catch her breath after climbing the stairs.

Oh boy, lots of time left in this pregnancy to be this winded already.

As she approaches her desk, she's greeted by a pile of papers waiting to be graded.

How am I going to handle working and raising two kids when I'm barely managing now?

Like a snowball, this one stressor sets off a series of more things she's been worrying about.

How will I split my time and affection between two children?

Will Drew feel neglected?

Will Allen feel neglected? We barely have time to be alone together now...

What if my marriage falls apart?

I should research marriage and parenting.

God, I hope they don't inherit my anxiety...

Stop it, crazy-pants. What would Dr. Hadley say to you right now?

Lucy imagines her therapist sitting calmly across from her and automatically feels her thoughts slow. She tucks her bag underneath her desk, takes a drink from her thermos and looks out her office window at the dark spring clouds. A blackbird flies past and lands in the closest tree. It has a twig in its mouth, and Lucy realizes it is building a nest.

Oh! Maybe there will be baby birds outside my window this year.

After watching the bird for a few minutes, she reluctantly returns her attention to preparing for her upcoming lesson. The topic is parenting styles and every year, it's a lesson that is always difficult for her to get through, both because of the memories it uncovers from her past and because it always causes her to question her own parenting.

Don't start thinking about it again. You already have a million times, and you have work to do.

She looks back out the window. Small rays of light are breaking through the dark clouds as she repeats a version of her familiar mantra.

You're not a bad mom.

You aren't messing your kid up.

He's healthy, and just as importantly, happy.

Relax.

The blackbird adds another twig to the nest before flying away. After another deep breath, she smiles, turns to her desk, and opens her laptop.

Eloise

Eloise holds her phone to her ear while she puts groceries away. On the other end, she can hear water running and dishes clinking occasionally in the sink.

Her mom asks, "Is the pregnancy going well?"

"Fine, I guess. I'm a little less tired now that I'm into the second trimester."

"Wow. I can't believe how fast that went." Her mom laughs loudly into the phone, and Eloise has to pull it away slightly. "Probably because you didn't tell me you were pregnant for so long!"

Eloise barely feels the slight dig. Her mom is a world-class travel agent for guilt trips.

Finished with the groceries, she sits down at the dining table and unconsciously starts doodling a wildflower field on one of the paper bags. She draws the silhouette of a woman standing amongst them while her mom continues talking.

"I loved being pregnant."

"You did?"

Genuine surprise makes her pause her drawing for a moment.

"Oh yeah, I loved how my skin glowed. I didn't love gaining weight of course. I felt like a whale. They say, 'eat for two' and I did! Took me forever to lose the weight from your sister." Her mom laughs. "Did I ever tell you that after your grandma had me, she would exercise and wear a trash bag under her clothes so that she would sweat off more weight?"

"That seems unhealthy."

Is she giving me a suggestion or something...?

"She got the idea from her sister. I think she said it worked pretty well for both of them if you need ideas for later."

Wow....

Her mom continues before she can respond.

"Oh- I meant to ask you. We're rearranging some furniture and I'm going to get rid of the rocking chair in the living room. Do you want it for the baby's room? I thought it might be nice for you to use."

"Sure. Thanks."

"And one more thing. I have an appointment in the city next week. Do you mind going with me? Your dad can't and I don't want to drive myself."

Eloise hears Parker coming inside. She catches his frown and senses his bad mood before she even fully sees him.

"I gotta go, Mom. Text me when the appointment is so I can check my schedule."

She ends the call, turning her attention to him. She watches as he rips off his muddy boots, leaving them dripping on the floor. He walks to the bathroom.

Eloise sighs.

Back to living with Oscar the Grouch.

She scribbles out her drawing, crumples up the bag and throws it away. She glances at the clock as she stands up.

She goes to the pantry and starts taking out cans for dinner. Over their clattering, she hears her text message alert and opens it to read a message from her mom with her appointment information.

"What's for dinner?" Parker asks as he walks into the living room to turn on the TV.

"Chili."

She hears *The Simpsons* come on as she opens a can of beans. She sets the phone down but leaves the message up as a reminder to check her calendar later.

Parker calls out from the couch, "Any chance you have some biscuits too?"

"No... I didn't buy any."

"Course not," he grumbles. She waits a moment.

"Can I get you something to drink?"

Like a beer?

She directs an overly deadpan face at the stove.

"A beer."

Called it.

Eloise goes to the fridge, opens the can and silently delivers it to him. She returns to the kitchen without a thank you, not that she was expecting one.

"How was your day?" she asks hesitantly.

"Fine."

She continues to cook dinner while he watches TV. When it's done, she scoops a few ladlefuls into a bowl before delivering it to him.

"Do you want some cheese? I forgot to put it on top."

"Sure."

Eloise senses his mood has improved now, slightly.

She brings the bag of shredded cheddar over to him and sprinkles some on top. Parker looks up at her and smiles.

"Thanks, sweets."

As she walks away, she sees the boots laying by the door. She hesitantly asks, "Could you maybe wipe up the mud from your boots after dinner?"

Through a mouthful of food and with a tone of distraction, Parker replies, "Yeah."

She gets her own bowl and sits beside him on the couch.

"Shoot, I forgot my water."

She pauses for a minute, waiting to see if he will get the subtle hint.

Wishful thinking.

She sighs as she sets the bowl on the coffee table to get her cup herself.

As Eloise reaches for the water cup, her vision sparkles and she sees a masculine hand lifting the cup up to hand it to her. She blinks and sees the cup in her hands, with no memory of picking it up. She drops it in surprise and watches water spread across the dining room table. Eloise rushes to pull the dish towel from its hook before the liquid spills to the floor. She looks back up and realizes Parker's eyes never even left the TV screen.

Lucy

Later that morning, Lucy and Angela head to the nearest off-campus cafe. It's been raining all week and though it's mostly cleared up, it's still a dreary, chilly day. A light drizzle has made their jackets misty. While they walk, they discuss how their semester classes are going. Angela's classes within the Native American Studies Department enthrall Lucy and she asks her question after question.

They stop at the crosswalk, waiting for the late morning traffic to pass. Once clear, they cross the street to the city's downtown. Students bustle by and around them, some in chatty groups and others with their heads down and buried in their phones. They push open the doors of the cafe and warmth instantly greets them, followed by the smell of freshly ground coffee and sweet baked goods.

Lucy recognizes the student working the counter from one of her classes. "Hi, Dr. Green! What can I get you today?"

Lucy smiles in greeting and orders an iced latte with the usual level of pretension.

Angela looks at her like she's crazy. "Iced? With today's weather?"

"I'll explain in a minute."

They both finish their orders and find a seat in the crowded shop. They carefully pull out their chairs so they don't disturb the students studying around them. When they sit down, Angela looks at her curiously and expectantly.

"So…. I'm pregnant. Most days only iced coffee sounds good."

"Oh, of course! Congratulations! I was so worried about you that day I saw you in the hall."

Lucy laughs. "Yeah, super glad you didn't come check on me."

"I hope you've been feeling better lately." At Lucy's nod, Angela continues. "Are your parents excited about another grandbaby?"

Such an innocent question.

"Um." Lucy looks at Angela's cheerful face before looking down. She twists her wedding band.

Should I tell her? And how much should I tell her?

After a few unpleasant encounters, she has learned to only tell those she knows she can trust and that will treat her with kindness rather than judgment.

I don't know Angela that well.

And I'm too tired to have this conversation today.

"I don't have parents anymore."

Not really a lie...

Angela replies sympathetically, "I'm so sorry."

The barista calls out their orders. "I'll get it for you." Angela quickly stands up before Lucy can move a muscle.

Lucy readjusts in her seat while she waits. She puts one leg on top of the other and gently bounces her foot.

Angela returns and places a scone dusted with powdered sugar in front of Lucy.

"Your student said to give this to you. She said it's on the house."

"Awe, so sweet!" Lucy looks toward the counter and makes eye contact with her. She mouths "Thank you" and both smile.

"Do you think it's a bribe to give her a good grade, though?"

Angela laughs. "Maybe."

"Want to split it with me?" Lucy gestures to the plate.

"Sure, thanks. I'll ask her for a knife."

As Angela stands up again, Lucy gets a text from Allen.

"Last minute meeting scheduled at work. Can you get Drew today?"

Lucy sighs and replies briefly, hoping he senses her passive aggressiveness. "Yes."

I wanted to finish reading those papers this afternoon...

Angela sits back down and, seeing her frown, asks if something is wrong.

"No, not really. Allen and I have to swap pickup today, so I have to reorganize my plans."

Angela nods understandingly. Lucy texts Allen again.

"Can you put Drew to bed tonight so I can finish grading?"

She sets her phone aside and asks, "How do you manage with four kids?"

Angela laughs. "I don't. I've just lowered my expectations WAY low." She takes a bite of the scone, swallowing before continuing. "I remind myself that this is just one season of life too, and it's a really busy one."

Lucy nods slowly.

"And when none of that works, I pop open a bottle of wine."

Lucy laughs. "Great idea."

Maybe I can ask Allen to start grocery shopping.

Does it really matter if he buys the wrong brand of peanut butter?

She takes a bite of the scone, feeling just a bit lighter.

Eloise

Eloise stands in the aisle of the local grocery store.

Ultra Strong.

Ultra Soft.

Ultra Soft AND Strong.

Her eyes scan the toilet paper shelves.

Where's the off brand to the bear one?

Ah ha. There.

"Eloise?"

She turns around and sees one of her childhood friends, Kate, standing in the aisle.

"Hey, how are you?" Eloise asks.

She self-consciously looks down at her jeans and sweater and compares them to her old friend's designer-looking clothes. She can't tell if they actually are, because she doesn't know what brands are designer. What she does know is that Kate looks a hundred times more put together than she does. And *of course* she would meet her in the toilet paper aisle as she's holding the cheapest mega-rolls.

"Good! My husband and I came home to visit. We left the kids with my parents so we could sneak out for dinner. He's wandering around somewhere. We had to come get a few things we forgot at home."

Eloise glances into her basket and sees a travel-sized bottle of face wash mixed with a colorful assortment of kid snacks.

All name-brand.

"Where are you living now?"

"We found jobs in metro-Detroit after college and have been there ever since."

And I'm still here... doing my grocery shopping at the same store we bought fudgesicles at in high school.

Eloise sees Kate glance at her belly. She has just started showing. She thinks about telling Kate she's pregnant but decides not to in order to avoid answering any follow-up questions.

Especially ones about the father...

"What do you do for work?" Eloise asks instead.

"I started an interior design company. I worked for a few companies before that, but I really wanted more flexibility after we had kids. How about you?"

Eloise hesitates, trying to figure out a way to make her life sound more exciting. She can't come up with a lie quick enough, though.

"I work at Frank Accounting."

"Wow. I'm surprised they didn't go out of business when H and R Block opened all those years ago."

Eloise laughs. "Me too honestly. And some days it shouldn't be open probably."

Kate laughs too as Eloise sees a man walking towards them. Kate looks towards what has caught Eloise's attention.

"Hey, hun. Eloise, this is Trey. Trey, this is Eloise. We were friends in high school."

"Hi, Eloise." Trey holds out his hand and smiles kindly at her. She can't help but notice that he's attractive.

He would look like that, like he could be on the cover of GQ.

"We should get going, Katie. It'll be time to get the kids to bed soon."

"Yeah, you're right. So good to see you, Eloise!"

"You too!"

Kate turns to go. She waves when she gets to the end of the aisle before grabbing Trey's hand. Eloise puts the toilet paper in her shopping cart and avoids making eye contact with anyone else for the rest of her shopping trip.

As she's putting her groceries away, she thinks about her run-in with Kate. She hasn't thought about her in a long time. They were pretty good friends in high school. They had a few classes together but really bonded in art class. Kate was talented, so Eloise isn't surprised that she picked a career where she could be creative.

Bet their house is amazing. She probably doesn't have a single foot of cheap linoleum in it.

Magazine quality living rooms and kitchens float through her mind. She takes the spaghetti noodles from the bag and turns to the pantry to put them away.

Some paint would freshen these cupboards up...

Eloise pictures different colors as she empties the rest of the grocery bag-moody gray, crisp white, mushroom brown...

Again, her mind fills with a clear vision of a different kitchen, a different house. The cabinets are a trendy blue, and she can smell cookies baking. The modern light fixtures above her give off a soft glow. Unexpectedly, the lights flash and the harsh dome lights in her own kitchen replace them. She stops and stands still to regain her sense of reality.

What the fuck is happening to me?

Her heart races, and she tries to slow her breathing.

You need to tell your doctor, Einstein.

She shuts the cupboard door and takes out her phone, making a note on her calendar.

I should go to bed earlier tonight too.

Lucy

Dr. Burman, Lucy's OB, knocks on the door and enters the bright room wearing her usual sunny smile. "Hi, Lucy. Good to see you again, Allen."

"You too. Lucy told me she heard the heartbeat last time, and I didn't want to miss out."

"Let's not waste time then, huh?" Dr. Burman prepares the monitor. She takes the gel out of the warmer and squeezes some onto Lucy's belly.

Lucy holds her breath as the doctor moves the wand across her skin, searching.

Why is it taking so long to find...?

Just as she's about to ask if things are okay, Dr. Burman stops her hand. Lucy hears the reassuring clipping noise.

Thank God.

"Nice and strong."

Dr. Burman smiles at them. Lucy turns to Allen and sees the emotion welling in his eyes. She grabs his hand.

Dr. Burman lets them listen for a few more seconds before removing the device and returning to her stool.

"I have your results back from the quad test we ordered last time."

Lucy senses a change in the doctor's tone.

Oh no, it's bad news. I knew it.

Her heart races while she waits for the doctor's next words.

"The results were inconclusive."

Shit.

Allen squeezes her hand tightly.

"What does that mean for us?" Lucy asks, panic beginning to raise the pitch of her voice.

"It could mean nothing. It was likely an error in the sample collection or testing. To be safe, we could run further tests, though."

Lucy answers immediately, "Yes, definitely."

I need to know how bad this is.

"Okay, I thought you'd say that. I'll get the order written up, and you can take it with you today. Try not to worry about it. I know that's easier said than done." Dr. Burman gently smiles at them before looking down to write on her clipboard.

Lucy turns to Allen and sees worry etching his features, too. He squeezes her hand again, and she notices it's become slightly sweaty.

If Allen is worried...

"We'll call you with the results, so you'll have them before your next appointment, okay? You'll actually have your ultrasound between now and then, so we can follow up on that at your appointment, too."

"Great. Thank you," Allen says.

"Do you have any questions or anything else you wanted to talk about today?" Lucy shakes her head no. Dr. Burman hands her the lab order and continues. "Okay. Please let us know if anything comes up before then. Have a good rest of your day."

Lucy stares blankly at the papers in her hand.

I knew this was all too good to be true.

I shouldn't have gotten my hopes up.

Seeing that Lucy can't reply, Allen says for them, "Thanks. You too."

Dr. Burman shuts the door. Allen turns to Lucy and rubs her back. Lucy's eyes fill up with tears. He pulls her closer and holds her tightly.

"We'll figure it out. We always do," he says quietly.

She squeezes Allen back, still unable to speak. Her tears create large, dark circles on his shirt.

Oh Baby....

Eloise

Eloise takes a deep breath, steadying herself, as she scrolls through her contact list. The week she's been dreading is nearly here.

"Hello?" Eloise's mom always answers the phone with a question to her tone, as if her cell phone doesn't have caller ID.

"Hi."

"Hey, hun! How are you?"

"Fine. I forgot to tell you. I saw Kate Webber at the grocery store."

"Oh really? She was always so cute, not pretty, but cute."

She said that about her in high school too.

A lot of moms would probably never say that about their child's friend...

She considers saying something but ignores it instead.

"She owns an interior design company."

"Good for her. Is she married? Does she have kids?"

Eloise rolls her eyes.

"Yes, to both."

"Well, that's nice. How's the baby?"

"Fine, I guess. That's why I'm calling, though." Eloise's mouth has gone dry, so she swallows uncomfortably before continuing. "Would you want to come with me to my ultrasound next week?"

"What day?"

"Tuesday."

The one weekday you said you could come.

"Oh. I'll be the only one in the office that day who can answer the phones..."

"There isn't anyone else in the office that day?"

"Well, Joanna will be there."

"She can't answer a phone…?"

"Ha! You'd think right?"

Eloise waits for her mom to say more, but she doesn't.

"So, you can't come?"

"No. Probably not."

"It's fine."

But it isn't really.

"Parker can't come?"

"No." She doesn't add that she didn't even think it was worth asking him.

Eloise's eyes tear up, and she wipes at them with the back of her hand.

"I have to go, Mom."

Her mom must hear her tone of disappointment because she says, "Now I feel bad! I wish you'd told me sooner."

"It's fine. I'll talk to you later."

"Okay, let me know how the appointment goes."

Eloise hangs up the phone without responding to her mom's last statement, a weak attempt to convey her hurt feelings.

I hope you never feel this alone, baby.

Her thoughts spin as she remembers the ticking time bomb she's carrying.

What happens when I need help in a few months?

Who will I call in the middle of the night?

Or when the baby is sick?

Or if I just need a break?

Mom will be more willing to help then....right?

Eloise considers their history for a moment, struck by sadness when she realizes she can't answer with a definite "yes."

Sometimes I feel like a piece of furniture in her life.

She makes a mental note to ask Sarah if she likes children or if she's at least willing to hold a baby long enough for Eloise to shower.

Eloise looks down and realizes she has absentmindedly doodled on the electric bill envelope. A tree branch stretches out from the left side of the page. A nest holding a speckled egg rests on it precariously.

Lucy

Lucy sits on her therapist's cushy teal velvet couch. The warm lamps and cream walls temper the boldness of the color. A plush rug and big, leafy green plants provide added softness, allowing those who sit in this room to feel more at ease. Details Lucy noticed on her first visit and ones that only a fellow psychologist would pick up on.

"How are you today, Lucy?"

"I'm okay. I've been better, honestly."

She's been seeing Dr. Violet Hadley for several years and she's been her favorite therapist by far.

"What's going on?"

Lucy sees Dr. Hadley's eyes soften with concern through her black cat eye glasses.

"I had a doctor appointment last week, and we didn't hear the results we were expecting from our quad screening." Lucy absentmindedly rubs her stomach. She pauses slightly before finishing with, "It isn't terrible, but they were inconclusive."

"I'm sorry to hear that. What are the next steps?"

Lucy tells her about the additional tests and ultrasound.

"So you have to wait. I know how much you don't enjoy waiting." Dr. Hadley smiles at Lucy.

"Yeah, I hate it." Lucy smiles back halfheartedly.

"How are you feeling about the situation?"

Lucy takes a deep breath and sighs. She twists her bracelets and stares into space as she thinks. Dr. Hadley sits patiently with her.

"A lot of things. Scared. Worried. Impatient. Stressed. Helpless…"

"Helpless. Like you have no control over it?"

"Exactly."

"Remember, we can't always control the situation, but we have some control over our responses."

"I know." Lucy sighs. "I'm trying to remind myself of that."

"What have you been saying to yourself?"

Lucy pauses as she considers this question.

"Mostly, that everything always works out. My husband tells me that all the time when I'm stressed about something."

Dr. Hadley smiles and passes the tissue box closer to her. "How often are you thinking about the tests or results?"

"A lot. Throughout the entire day."

"How about if we set a time where you allow yourself to worry? Schedule 10-15 minutes a day to consider your worries and if you find them creeping into your thoughts at other times, tell yourself you'll think about it in your next worry session."

"I'd be willing to try it."

"Good. I know this situation isn't easy and that it's hard to feel so helpless. By scheduling time, it may help you establish a sense of control over your thoughts and anxiety."

They discuss specifics and come up with a plan for Lucy to try.

"Anything else you want to discuss today?"

She remembers the note she made in her phone for today's appointment.

"Yes… the visions are back, just like when I was pregnant with Drew."

Dr. Hadley's eyes widen slightly, a change from her usually cool, collected demeanor.

Probably should have led with that I guess…

"How often are they happening?"

"Not that often, a few over the last couple of months."

Or maybe more…I don't want to go back on that medication, though.

"I know your body didn't react well to the antipsychotic last pregnancy."

Lucy sees flashes of an emergency room visit.

Beeping monitors attached to her belly.

An IV pinching her skin.

Nurses rushing around her.

A doctor shouting orders.

Dr. Hadley continues, "I don't want to prescribe anything without talking to your OB first. Have you talked to her yet?"

"No. I wanted to tell you first."

"Have you told Allen?"

"No. I don't want to worry him." Lucy adds quickly, "I think I have some control over them, and they really haven't happened that often."

Yet.

I can't go through that again though, and the medication didn't even stop them from happening last time.

Maybe they aren't hallucinations...?

Her therapist stares at her closely over her glasses, assessing her.

"Okay... Please let me or your OB know though if anything changes, especially if they become more frequent or intense." She softens her look and tone. "We can figure something out together. I think you should tell Allen, too."

Lucy sighs, "Okay."

If they aren't hallucinations, then what are they?

* * *

Forty-five minutes later, Lucy walks in their front door and hears Allen and Drew playing in the living room. She pauses in the doorway and watches them silently until Allen looks up and sees her.

"Hey! Look who's home." He picks Drew up and carries him over to Lucy. Lucy kisses Drew on the forehead.

"I brought Thai food home for dinner tonight."

"I'll get the plates ready. You can spend some time with Drew."

"Thanks, hun." Allen kisses her cheek before picking up the takeout bag she left in the entryway.

She breathes out in relief once he leaves the room.

I know I need to tell him, but I really don't want to. Neither of us needs more stress right now.

She scoops up Drew and asks, "How was your day, buddy?"

"Good! We jumped in puddles!"

"Fun! Who did you play with today?"

Lucy sits on the couch with Drew, snuggling him tight as he tells her about his day. There is no drama she'd rather listen to than who wasn't at daycare today or which of his friends fell down and hurt themselves.

"Dinner's all set," Allen says softly from the doorway.

She looks up and sees him leaning against the wall quietly, smiling as he watches and listens to them. She lets Drew finish his story as she carries him into the dining room for dinner, adjusting him so he rests around her bump.

She sets him down in his seat, and he looks at his plate.

"Aww. Dammick! I thought I was having apples!"

Lucy and Allen look at each other with wide eyes. Allen mouths "dammick?"

Both of them stifle laughter but choose to ignore the word for now. Meanwhile, Drew has already started eating his oranges.

"Guess we'll have to be more careful about what we say," Allen mutters to her.

Lucy's eyes crinkle with a smile, forgetting her concerns for now. "Wonder how many times he's said that at daycare."

Eloise

The TV blasts loudly, some show that Parker has picked and that Eloise doesn't really care for. They are sitting on the couch together. Eloise has covered herself in her afghan and has her feet resting on Parker's lap. Now and then, he rubs her feet and legs. His mood has been a little lighter this evening.

"How was your day?" she asks, testing the waters.

"Fine. How was yours?"

"Also fine. Nothing too exciting."

"Did you go shopping already?" he asks her.

"Yes, why?"

"I need more shampoo. I forgot to tell you."

You could get your own shampoo like an adult...

Don't say that and upset him, though.

"I can pick some up tomorrow."

Parker watches TV while Eloise delays what she wants to ask next. All day long she has been feeling butterflies in her stomach.

Finally, she hesitantly asks, "Will you come to my ultrasound appointment with me on Tuesday?"

Parker's eyes don't leave the TV screen.

"This Tuesday? Like three days from now?"

"Yeah."

He stops rubbing her leg and she sees his jaw tighten.

"I can't ask my boss for the day off now. You should have asked sooner if you wanted me to come."

106

Eloise looks down at the blanket and pulls it tighter against herself.

He's right. I should have.

"I didn't think you'd want to..."

"I don't. I didn't want this baby in the first place."

An intense desire to protect her child rises within her. She responds before attempting to predict his reaction.

"But *I* do. What are you going to do when the baby comes?" Eloise asks sharply.

Like a lit match, she sees Parker's anger instantly mirror her own- his breath quickens, nostrils flare slightly, cheeks redden...

Shit.

"What are you suggesting?"

Eloise lowers her voice. "I don't know. Forget I said anything."

She rises quickly and exits the room.

What will *he do when the baby comes?*

Act like the baby doesn't exist when he's here?

Yell all the time?

Or be gone more than he already is?

She brushes her teeth and walks into the bedroom.

As she slips beneath her worn quilt, the butterflies she's been feeling all day suddenly turn into larger, foreign movements.

Is that...the baby moving...?

She lays quietly for a few moments, analyzing the unfamiliar sensations.

It's like popcorn popping in there...

Eloise feels overcome with loneliness.

It's just you and me, baby.

The movements eventually slow and then stop.

If he doesn't leave, can I...? Should I?

The logistics of that feel too overwhelming to solve right now.

Maybe things will get better between us once the baby comes.

Maybe...

She finally falls asleep with salty lines dried on her face.

Lucy

Lucy smiles as she looks at her new phone background, an ultrasound image of her baby.

So glad that everything looked okay.

I just hope the doctor agrees...

She texts Allen, "My next patient canceled. Do you want to grab a quick lunch?"

That would give us some uninterrupted time to talk.

Allen replies, and they agree on the details.

Fifteen minutes later, Lucy arrives at one of their favorite restaurants, a hippie brewpub with the best organic berry cobbler. She orders them both waters and as the waitress is bringing them to the table, Allen walks in with his typical calming smile. Lucy feels some of her tension evaporate.

I love this guy.

Lucy scans the diverse menu, and they make small talk about their mornings. After she orders a falafel burger with pickled onions, she sips her water, spilling some down her pale floral top.

I wish this place used straws, but apparently they're bad for the environment.

Something about sea turtles.

She dabs her shirt with a napkin and remembers why she asked to have lunch together.

"I have to tell you something." Allen looks up quickly and waits for her to say more. "Remember the visions I had when I was pregnant with Drew?"

Like he could forget...

"They're back?" he asks worriedly.

Lucy purses her lips slightly and nods.

"When did they start this time?"

"A couple months ago, but I haven't had many."

"A couple months? Why didn't you tell me sooner?" Lucy can see the slight hurt in his eyes.

"I don't know. I didn't want to worry you."

"Lucy, we've talked about this so many times. You don't have to protect me."

"I know..." She meets Allen's eyes, smiling at the tenderness she sees reflecting at her.

"Are you going to tell your doctor?"

"I told Dr. Hadley and promised her I'd tell her and my OB if they get worse."

"Okay, good. Has Dr. Burman's office contacted you with the test results?"

"No, not yet... If it was bad news we'd have heard something by now, right?"

As if on cue, her phone rings. She plans on letting it go to voicemail so they can finish their date but changes her mind when she sees the caller.

Oh no.

"It's the doctor's office." She looks at Allen with tense eyes as she accepts the call. He reaches his hand across the table, and she places hers on top.

"Hello?" she asks hesitantly.

"Hi, is this Lucy?"

"Yes."

"This is Nurse Rachel. I'm calling to follow up with your test results."

Lucy breathes in a deep breath, waiting for more.

"The results all came back normal. Dr. Burman specifically told me to tell you that now you can worry less."

Lucy finally exhales with her reply, "Thank you. So much."

She looks up at Allen. He smiles broadly and his eyes glisten.

"She said she'll talk with you more at your next appointment but wanted to give you some good news before then."

"Thank you," Lucy repeats. "See you then."

"Have a great rest of your day!"

"You too."

Lucy ends the call and places her free hand on her stomach. She lets her relieved tears flow freely. Allen squeezes her hand and wipes his own eyes.

Her daughter kicks lightly against her palm.

Eloise

Eloise waits at her small-town hospital for her ultrasound, alone. She nervously adjusts in her seat every few minutes. The room is full of other patients, most sitting beside a loved one.

"All by myself, don't wanna be..."

The corners of her mouth turn up in a sad smile as the middle-aged ultrasound tech finally comes into the waiting room to collect her.

"My name is Pam. We'll go right this way," she says as she leads Eloise down a hallway.

"How are you today?" the tech asks.

Excited. Scared. Nauseous. Lonely.

Way too much info for Pam.

"I'm alright."

"How's the weather? Is it still raining?"

Why do people insist on making small talk for these kinds of things?

"It's still cloudy, but the rain has stopped."

They finally come to a dark room.

"That's good. It was raining cats and dogs out when I came in."

Pam gestures to the chair for Eloise to sit. She presses a button, and the chair reclines so that now she's lying down. "Were you hoping to find out the gender today?"

Pam looks at her with a warm smile on her face.

"Oh, um." *Was I...?* "Yes. Please."

"Okay. We're going to take a lot of pictures for measurements, too. Let's hope Baby is cooperative for all of them."

Eloise watches the screen as the technician moves the probe across her stomach. Now and then she clicks to take a picture and the screen freezes. One of these times it stops on a tiny, blurry face.

"There's your baby."

Pam looks from the screen to Eloise, but Eloise's throat is too tight to respond. Pam notices and hands her a tissue.

"What a cutie pie, huh? Is this your first?"

"Yeah," Eloise replies breathlessly.

Pam moves the probe a little more and snaps another picture. She smiles happily back at Eloise. "That will be a nice one for you to keep."

She continues to move the probe around, attempting to find something. Clearly she knows what she's looking for because Eloise can't tell what anything is. Pam pushes the probe a little harder, nudging the baby gently.

"Just move a little, Baby…." Pam mutters. "There we go."

She stops and takes another picture.

"And… It's a girl."

Eloise can't contain her emotion this time. Pam hands her another tissue as tears overflow from her eyes. The image on the screen shakes slightly, and Eloise feels a tiny push against her stomach.

"Oh! And there's a kick. She's a little bit feisty," Pam says.

Pam and Eloise laugh.

The realization that she is seeing her baby in real time suddenly hits Eloise. She takes a moment and stares at the screen incredulously.

There is an actual human INSIDE of me.

And I'm sharing this magical moment with an absolute stranger.

More tears flow from her eyes, familiar loneliness mixing with this foreign joy.

"Isn't it amazing that we can capture a tiny peek into their world before they come into ours?"

Unbelievable.

"Just a few more pictures and measurements and we should be all set. I haven't been able to get a good look at her heart yet. Why don't you try laying on your other side to see if she'll move."

Eloise turns over and Pam continues to push the wand around her abdomen gently for several more minutes.

"Hmm. She's being stubborn. I think I'll have you take a walk to see if that will get her to turn for me."

"What if you can't see what you need to?" Eloise asks nervously.

What if there's something wrong and they can't tell?

"The doctor will look at the images and will determine if you should come back in for additional ones."

More time off. How much personal time do I have left?

As Eloise stands up to tour the building, she thinks back to the doctor offering her the genetic screening test. She waited too long and now the time limit is up for it. The next 15 minutes pass agonizingly slowly as she walks up and down the stairs, and up and down the stairs, and up and down the stairs, thoughts looping with regret at her indecision.

You can't go back now, so you may as well get over it.

She checks her phone again. 13 minutes.

Close enough.

She walks down the stairs one last time and re-enters the dark room.

Pam watches her enter and brightly says, "Alright! Let's try again!"

Her enthusiasm does little to lighten Eloise's worry that something could be wrong. Pam continues to move the probe again and several minutes pass in silence. Eloise's anxiety doubles.

"Hmm. I don't think Baby wants to cooperate."

Eloise waits for Pam to say more.

Please move a little. I just want to know you're okay.

"Is there anything else I can do so you can see what you need better?"

Pam pushes the wand a little harder, but Eloise can see her daughter hasn't budged.

"I think she's pretty comfy today." Pam puts the device back on the cart. "I'll send what I have to your doctor, and we'll see what he says. Here are a couple of prints for you to take home and a CD of the rest."

Pam hands her the items.

"Thank you."

Eloise stares at her daughter's blurry face, at her perfectly curved nose and slightly pouty lips. She turns to the next image and five tiny fingers wave back at her, followed by an image of her two small feet. She says a silent prayer, asking that everything is okay.

From now on, I will do better for you.

Lucy

Early morning light streams through the kitchen. Lucy looks through the windows at the bright green lawn and smiles.

Welcome back, sunshine. I missed you, old friend.

She yawns as she sets her mug on the counter and takes out some coffee beans to grind. She fills the teapot with water and turns on the stove, wanting to get caffeine into her system as quickly as possible.

As her belly grows larger, getting comfortable enough to sleep is a challenge.

The middle of the night Charley Horses aren't helping either.

She measures the beans, dumps them into the grinder and the abrasive sound fills the kitchen. As she shakes the grounds into the French press, Drew calls for them from his room, and she waits for Allen to get him. The teapot whistles, and when it really screams she hears Drew yell from the doorway, "Mama! Your coffee ready!"

"Thanks, honey." She smiles as she pours the steaming water into the coffee press. She walks over to her two favorite guys and gives each of them a kiss on the cheek. "How did you sleep, hun?"

"Good," Drew says.

"I slept well too. Thanks for asking." Allen winks and Lucy chuckles. She wrinkles her nose affectionately at Drew, then looks up at Allen. "Can you change his pull up while I get plates ready?"

"Sure. Let's go, buddy!"

Lucy puts a muffin on a plate for each of them and opens a banana for

Drew. She presses the top of the French press down slowly, but firmly. When it stops at the bottom, she carefully pours the steaming dark liquid into her cup. The smell of the freshly brewed coffee greets her nose.

Oh Mama, that's good.

She stirs in a little cream, coloring the coffee a warm caramel as Drew's feet patter back into the room. He pulls himself into the booster seat attached to the chair. Lucy watches to make sure he makes it safely but doesn't warn him to be careful this time. She sets his plate in front of him and widens her eyes as he takes a giant bite of muffin.

His cheeks bulge, and he says through a full mouth, "Yumm!"

She laughs, staring lovingly at his sweet face. Lucy brings her mug to the table, nestling herself into the quiet of this morning.

"What should we do today, bud?"

Drew sits up on his knees and stares at her, his chocolate eyes wide with excitement. "Can we go to the park?"

"That's a great idea."

They finish breakfast, and since it's nice out, load Drew into his stroller to walk to the park. When they arrive, it's mostly quiet. There's still a spring chill in the air and not everyone has stopped hibernating from the winter.

"What do you want to do first, buddy?" Lucy asks Drew.

"Swing!"

Allen sets Drew down and Lucy laughs as she watches him soar over to the swing set like a plane. His jacket flaps lightly behind him. Allen helps Drew into the swing and starts pushing him.

"Higher!" Drew shouts.

"You got it, little man."

Lucy spies a bench close to the swing set and takes this opportunity to rest her tired feet from the walk.

She smiles as the swing moves back and forth rhythmically and lets her eyes wander the rest of the playground.

Sliding down the toddler slide is a girl a little older than Drew. A woman Lucy assumes to be the girl's mom stands nearby, scrolling on her phone.

Lucy's eyes move to the larger play structure when she hears delighted squealing.

"No! Don't get me, Papa Bear!"

Two little boys race through the structure, turning their heads over their shoulders occasionally to look behind them.

"I'm coming for you!"

An older gentleman playfully lumbers after them. He catches Lucy watching and smiles at her.

She smiles back, but sadness touches the corners.

I know Drew doesn't seem to notice yet, but what happens when he realizes he doesn't have grandparents around much?

Like when he starts school and sees other kids' grandparents at events?

Allen's parents don't live close enough to come to everything...

"Mama!" Drew's call interrupts her thoughts, and she returns her gaze to him, fixing the smile on her face to hide the sadness. "Look how high!"

"You are so high!" Her gaze lingers on her son's face, joy radiating across his features.

That's a problem for future Lucy.

I just want to enjoy the park with my son right now.

"I done, Dad!"

She watches in horror as Drew lifts himself off the moving swing.

"Careful, Drew!" she calls out loudly.

"Luce, I have him," Allen says reassuringly, but Lucy thinks she hears a note of exasperation in his tone.

Or you're just projecting that onto him.

Allen gradually slows the swing and lifts Drew from it. Drew runs over to her and presses his small hands into her thighs.

"Mama, can you play with me?"

"Always, buddy."

She feels the warmth of his small hand in hers as he pulls her across the playground.

Eloise

A cool breeze drifts gently across her face as Eloise walks the downtown sidewalk to the hardware store. The grass has turned a vibrant green, and pink and white blossoms float through the air. Eloise is so focused on her mission she barely notices these things, purposefully distracting herself from her worried thoughts.

As she walks, she's reminded of just how much she feels like a penguin while her belly grows larger and the baby drops lower. Her feet ache.

Damn. I should have found a closer parking spot.

Didn't there used to be parking for pregnant women? What happened to those?

She glances in the window of the small pottery studio as she passes by, eyeing all the beautiful pieces on display. Hanging above them is a "Now Hiring" sign. She pauses and stares at it, imagining what it would be like to work in a pottery studio.

Ridiculous. That won't ever pay the bills.

She continues walking and enters the hardware store, heading directly to the paint aisle on her left.

She admires the rainbow of colors, the pain in her feet forgotten.

"Do you need any help, ma'am?"

A man about her age smiles kindly from the end of the aisle. His blue eyes seem to sparkle under the bright lights. He has a work apron tied around his neck and on his chest is a name badge.

Brian.

"I'm just browsing right now. Thank you, though."

"Let me guess- you're painting a nursery?"

She laughs as she places her hand on her stomach, now several inches higher than it used to be. "Lucky guess."

"Well, let me know if you need any help."

"Thank you." Eloise subconsciously glances at his left hand and notices that there's no ring.

He may be married and just not wear one, though, or at least dating someone.

And it doesn't matter right now, anyway. What are you even thinking?

She turns back to the display in front of her.

But when was the last time Parker made you laugh?

Eloise doesn't let herself think about that as she loses herself in the color swatches, comparing varying shades of pinks, purples, grays, yellows... She holds three cards with slightly distinct blush shades up to the light.

"Those are nice."

She has been so absorbed in picking out colors she didn't hear the elderly woman enter the aisle.

"I think so, too," Eloise replies.

"Are you having a girl, then?"

Eloise nods and smiles at the stranger. The woman smiles back at her and points towards the samples. As she does, Eloise notices a blackbird charm hanging from the bracelet on her wrist.

"I like the one on the top right."

Eloise looks at the samples in her hand.

"Me too. Thanks." She smiles back at the woman.

"You're welcome." The woman turns to leave and waves goodbye, causing the charm to jingle.

Eloise replaces the other cards and heads to the register to order the paint.

Once one is filled, she picks up the can to test its weight.

Can I carry both of these to my car in one trip?

As she moves the can up and down a few inches, Brian asks her, "Would you like some help taking these cans out?"

Eloise looks up and smiles. He returns it and she feels the baby flutter (*at least I think that's the baby...*).

"That'd be great. Thanks so much."

After she checks out, Eloise walks back to her car so she can move it closer for Brian to help her load the paint. As she walks by the pottery studio, she sees the hiring sign again. She stops and enters the number into her phone. *Just so I have it.*

She feels the baby kicking sharply against her stomach, leaving her with no doubt that it was her this time.

Lucy

"Good morning, beautiful!" Allen says softly.

Drew stands in the doorway, and Allen enters the bedroom behind him carrying a tray. A steaming mug of coffee and a plate of scrambled eggs and berries rests on it.

Drew races over to the bed and raises his arms to be picked up.

"Happy Mutter Day!"

"Aww. Thanks, buddy. Did you guys make breakfast for me?"

"Yeah! We made coffee! And eggs. And berries."

"My favorite! Thank you!" She kisses the top of his messy head.

Allen sets the tray on the bed, and Lucy notices Drew eyeing her berries greedily.

"These look delicious. Would you like one?"

"Yes, please." She picks up a strawberry with her fork and extends it to him.

"Drew, you already ate breakfast!" Allen says to him.

He chews the strawberry and smiles happily at his mom.

"I still hungry."

Allen shakes his head. He sets a present on the bed.

"Do you want to give your mom her gift?"

"Yes! Here!" Drew pushes the gift bag into Lucy's lap.

"I help open it?"

"Sure, hun."

Lucy unwraps the gift. Drew "helps" by pulling all the tissue paper out and throwing it messily around the bed.

Inside is a white canvas tote bag. On the front are tiny yellow handprints

121

forming a sun. Delicate brushstrokes read, "You are my sunshine."

"Oh! I love it!" Lucy looks at it closely before wrapping Drew in a big hug. "Who helped you make this?"

"My teacher!"

"You did a great job. Thanks, buddy."

"You welcome. Can I have another berry?"

"Drew!" Allen says.

Lucy laughs and picks a plump red strawberry for him. "Sure, hun."

As she hands it to him, she notices his nose is runny and she grabs a tissue from beside the bed.

"Let me wipe your nose."

"Ah! No!" He tries to scramble away, but despite her belly in the way, Lucy miraculously catches him.

She turns to Allen, "I'm worried he's getting sick."

"It's probably just a cold."

"Probably. Can you find the baby vapor rub and get out the humidifier in case he needs it?"

After breakfast, Lucy sits on the couch while Drew plays with his toys in the living room. Sunlight pours through the windows, comfortably warming the room.

She sends a quick text to her sister. "Happy Mother's Day, Sis! Hope you have a great day and that your family makes you feel special! You deserve it."

Lucy sets her phone back down and rubs her stomach. She has been feeling uncomfortable all morning with the baby resting underneath her ribs. She pushes lightly on her stomach to see if she will readjust. Drew starts coughing, which quickly turns into a fit he has trouble stopping.

"Whoa, buddy. Come get a drink of water." Lucy hands him his cup and continues pressing on her daughter with her other hand.

Drew sees his mom rubbing her stomach and comes to stand beside her.

"Hi, sister. It me..." Drew deepens his voice. "The Hulk!" He squares his shoulders and swaggers around the room. Lucy laughs and in response to either her brother or mom, the baby kicks excitedly.

"Look, Drew! Your sister is saying hello back!"

Drew runs over and stares at Lucy's wiggling stomach with wide eyes. "Cool, huh?"

Allen walks out from the kitchen and sits next to Lucy on the couch. He places his hand on her belly where it's moving and smiles as their daughter kicks him back. He looks at Lucy and warmly says,

"Happy Mother's Day."

She leans in to kiss him. "Thank you."

She rests her head on his shoulder while Drew plays on the floor, coughing occasionally. Allen's hand rests on her stomach and her daughter continues to wiggle and kick.

Wonder what my mom is doing today.

You could call her...

Lucy looks out the window and sees dark gray clouds forming in the distance. The sun shining makes them seem even darker and more ominous.

Not today. Today is about enjoying my little family.

Drew has another coughing spell. She hands him his water and asks Allen, "What did you do with the vapor rub? I want to put some on him."

Eloise

"Aww. Look how cute you are!"

Her mom hugs her as she and Parker come inside for the family's Mother's Day lunch. She pulls away and rubs Eloise's stomach.

Why does being pregnant suddenly make all social norms disappear? No one touches a woman's stomach like that when she isn't pregnant.

Her mom takes a card and gift bag from the table and hands both to her, "Happy Mother's Day."

"Thanks," she replies, pulling back. "I got you a hanging flower basket, your favorite-purple geraniums. We left it on the porch." Eloise points out the window.

Her mom glances out the door at the flowers. "They're beautiful." She smiles at Eloise as she turns back to continue cooking lunch.

I had to go to three greenhouses to find those, and she barely looked at them.

"It's nice to be appreciated by one daughter. I can't remember the last Mother's Day I even heard from your sister."

Eloise ignores the comment as she takes her jacket to the bedroom.

I'm still not her favorite, even when my sister hasn't spoken to her in years.

She hears her mom ask Parker if he got Eloise anything for Mother's Day.

Big fat nope.

"I thought I didn't have to until after the baby comes?"

Her mom laughs in response, always easily charmed by Parker.

I don't think it's funny and he should know that.

She masks any trace of emotion before leaving the bedroom.

When she returns, Parker is already sitting on the couch with her dad watching television.

"Why didn't you have Dad grill today, Mom?" she asks as she enters the kitchen.

"The weather wasn't very nice for it."

"We should have gotten pizza or something. You shouldn't have to cook on Mother's Day."

"Oh, it's fine. It's just another day really."

"I could have brought something." Eloise watches her mom buzz around the kitchen preparing the meal solo. "What can I help you with now?"

"I think I have everything all set."

She watches her mom stirring a pot with one hand while checking the oven timer with the other. Eloise shakes her head and rolls her eyes to herself.

"I'll go get the plates and utensils ready."

Her mom replies without looking up, "Okay, that would be good."

"I picked up some paint for the baby's room," Eloise says when she returns.

"What color did you pick?" Her mom eyes her curiously.

"… light pink."

"Yay! Does that mean you're having a girl?"

Eloise laughs. "Yes."

"I'm so excited. Little girl clothes are so cute."

Eloise finishes neatly stacking the paper plates and plastic cups on the counter. "I asked Parker if he could paint the room for me. He didn't really answer."

Parker overhears her and yells back, "You just asked a couple days ago. I haven't had time to respond."

Eloise ignores him and asks quieter, "If he doesn't do it, can you help me?"

"Yeah, probably. Or maybe your dad can help."

"Okay. Thanks."

"Do you have any names picked out?"

"No, I just found out."

"I always liked the name Genevieve, but your dad told me it was too old sounding."

Yeah…. Good call on Dad's part…. Glad I'm not a Genevieve.

"I don't think I'll be naming her Genevieve. I'm not having an 80-year-old. Thanks for the suggestion, though."

"Oooh. How about Cordelia?"

Oh boy...

She feels her daughter kick lightly, followed by a small cramp. It isn't the first time this has happened, and like the other times, it is mild and brief.

Is that normal? I'll ask the doctor.

Lucy

Drew's cold has gotten worse. He's been lying on the couch for the last twenty-four hours and napping off and on.

He's normally like the Energizer Bunny.

Lucy sits beside him and watches his chest contract tightly with every breath. The ibuprofen has worn off, causing his fever to creep back. She looks at Allen, worry in her eyes.

"I think we need to take him to the doctor. I'm worried he has RSV. It's going around daycare, and I looked up the symptoms and he has several..."

"Okay, do you want me to take him?"

"Let me call and see if they have any appointments right away tomorrow morning. Otherwise, we should take him to the urgent care tonight or tomorrow morning."

Lucy calls the doctor's after-hours number and schedules the first appointment available the following morning.

She listens as the doctor gives her the warning signs to watch for and urges her to take Drew to the ER that evening if they notice any of them.

Has he had any of those symptoms yet?

No, I'd have noticed.

When she returns to the living room, she sees Drew has fallen asleep again. Allen has moved so that his hand is resting on Drew's small back.

"I can stay out here with him tonight," he half-whispers.

"Are you sure?"

"Yeah, you should sleep in the bed. It will be more comfortable."

"That's sweet of you. Thank you."

* * *

After tossing and turning with worry about her son and feeling uncomfortable with her ever-growing stomach, Lucy is finally asleep but dreams fitfully.

She's had this dream before, and it is always so realistic it is hard for her to distinguish between it and reality when she wakes up. Nothing dramatic ever happens. It just seems like she is living her regular life... but a different one. She never knows the specific details like where exactly she lives or works. She always feels a deep sense of sadness and loneliness, though. As always, she is living in a different house from hers, one that is small and outdated. Allen and Drew are not there. She walks through the house, down the hallway and into a darkened bedroom.

Lying in the bed is a man. He snores loudly with an open mouth, and she can smell cheap beer on his breath. She quietly lies down next to him, feeling nauseated and disgusted. She's aware in her dream that she is trying hard not to wake him, but the man rolls over anyway and starts gently nudging her. She tries to ignore it, hoping he'll think she's sleeping, but instead he pushes her more aggressively.

Her eyes snap open and she realizes Allen is shaking her awake.

"Lucy, I think we need to take Drew to the hospital."

Her heart skips a beat as adrenaline and fear pool in her abdomen. Their weight makes it feel like her stomach has flipped upside down. She gets out of bed as quickly as her pregnant belly will allow her, still in between states of consciousness.

Eloise

Major RBF is back for Eloise's appointment today and greets her with the usual level of enthusiasm.

After she takes her vitals silently and leaves with a flat, "The doctor will be in soon," Eloise pulls out her phone. She's reading through the notes she's made when Dr. Sattler knocks and enters the drab room.

"How are you today, Eloise?"

"I'm alright."

"How have you been feeling?"

"Fine. I've had some cramping, though."

"It's probably just Braxton Hicks. It's your body's way of preparing for labor. Have you had any bleeding?"

"No, no bleeding. Something else has been happening that I wanted to ask you about." Eloise takes a deep breath. "A few times now I've had weird visions. It's hard to explain…"

Dr. Sattler waits for her to add more. When she doesn't, he asks, "Like daydreams or more like a hallucination?"

"Um, I'm not really sure. I don't know if they're either of those. They don't last long, a few seconds, and they haven't happened in a little while."

"Okay, you're probably just tired or dehydrated. Try to get more sleep and drink more water. Let me know if they become more frequent or intense though and we can go from there."

So if he isn't concerned, should I be?

Should HE be more concerned?

He's the doctor though, so he'd know right?

Eloise watches Dr. Sattler's face and sees him frown slightly.

Oh no...

"I got the results from your ultrasound, and I see they weren't able to get all the images we like to have."

"No, the baby didn't want to cooperate."

"And you didn't do the genetic screening tests that were offered, correct?"

"No..." Eloise pulls her sweater tight around herself and looks at the floor.

"Okay, I think we'll send you for one more ultrasound and some more bloodwork."

"Do you think something is wrong?"

"Not necessarily, but I'd like more information."

Is he not telling me something?

He finishes the lab order and then stands up so he can measure her stomach. He presses on her belly lightly and then prepares the heartbeat monitor.

"Okay. Let's take a listen." Eloise hears the foreign, yet now familiar galloping sound of her baby's heart. Dr. Sattler smiles.

"Still nice and strong." He lets her listen for a few more seconds and then hands her a paper towel to wipe off her stomach. He returns to his stool and writes a few notes on her chart.

"Do you have any questions?"

Eloise can't put her worries into answerable questions, so she simply says, "No."

"Okay, let us know if you do or if anything comes up. Have a good rest of your day."

"Thank you, you too."

She collects her things from the room and stops at the desk to schedule her ultrasound appointment. She doesn't allow herself to cry until she is safe in the privacy of her car. Her daughter kicks in response to her sobs.

It's okay. We're gonna be okay.

After several minutes, she has collected herself enough to drive safely, her daughter continuing to press closely against her.

Lucy

Lucy's brain is still buzzing from the chaos that started after they left their home. Fragmented scenes from the last few hours keep popping into her head.

Entering the empty waiting room.

Rushing to the check-in window while Allen stands behind her holding Drew.

The bright lights of the exam room.

The doctor's worried face.

Drew's pale skin and labored breathing.

His listless body...

He has to be okay.

Or I won't be.

She looks at him now, sleeping peacefully with an oxygen mask on his sweet face.

I can't lose him.

A nurse enters the room, hair pulled up in a messy bun. Despite the tiredness in her eyes, she smiles kindly at them.

"I have his test results back," she whispers to avoid waking Drew.

Lucy stands up and moves closer to her.

"They came back positive for RSV, and the doctor diagnosed him with bronchiolitis. It's good you brought him in. RSV can turn severe quickly."

Lucy releases her breath and thanks the nurse.

"What's next?" she asks.

"We'll keep monitoring his oxygen levels. Once we're confident with them, we'll remove the oxygen mask and see how his levels respond. We'll go from there."

"So he's going to be okay?"

The nurse hesitates but smiles. "He's responding well to the supports we've tried so far. I'll come check on him in a bit. Let us know if you need anything."

She walks silently from the room.

She didn't really answer my question.

The nighttime hours pass slowly. Lucy and Allen sit close by Drew's bed. Allen eventually falls asleep, his head resting uncomfortably on the back of the chair.

Lucy's eyes close heavily every so often before she jerks herself awake.

I can't sleep. I have to watch him to make sure he's okay.

Allen wakes up and notices her head bob one of these times.

"Hun, we're in a hospital. They're taking care of him. It's okay to get some rest."

"I can't," she whispers.

She looks back down at her son, feeling the warm weight of his small hand resting in hers.

Early morning light eventually brightens the sterile room. As she stares out the window, she looks out at the city below them. She smiles slightly as she thinks how happy Drew will be that they can see the train tracks.

Shoot, I was supposed to meet Bree for coffee today.

She reluctantly lets go of Drew's hand so she can send Bree a text canceling and explaining why. Expecting to not hear from her for awhile, Lucy reaches for Drew's hand again.

Surprisingly, her phone lights up after just a couple of minutes.

"What hospital and what time are visiting hours?"

Lucy replies and then asks why Bree is up so early.

"I have to study for an exam today."

"Good luck!"

Her gaze returns to Drew. His eyes move underneath his eyelids, and she notices that he's smiling. She smiles back and whispers a silent prayer of thanks before reluctantly drifting off to sleep.

* * *

"Knock knock." Lucy turns her head and sees Bree standing at the door with a to-go cup in one hand and a gift bag in the other.

"Aunt Bee!" Drew yells.

"Hey buddy, how are you?"

"I'm bored." Drew's lip pouts dramatically.

"You know, I thought you'd say that, so I brought you something."

Bree hands Drew the gift bag. He rips into it, littering tissue paper all over the hospital bed and floor. He pulls out a Transformer set.

"Cool!"

"These look fun, buddy." Allen helps Drew open the box, hands Drew the first figure and then takes another to play-fight with Drew's.

Bree smiles and hands Lucy the cup. "This is for you. I figured you'd need it, and I'm sure the hospital coffee isn't up to your standards."

Lucy takes a sip of the coffee and sighs, its smooth taste awakening her soul.

"Thanks. You're right though, it isn't. You didn't have to come. I thought you had an exam?"

"I already took it. I think it went well."

They watch Drew play for several seconds.

"How is he?"

"Much better, thankfully. The oxygen has helped."

"Good. I'm glad. How scary. I'm so sorry, Lucy."

"It was scary." Lucy's eyes water as the memory of her intense fear returns.

"Have they said how long they think you'll have to stay?"

"No, I'm hoping that he gets better quickly and that we can go home in the next day or so."

Allen stands up and stretches. "I think I may go home for a bit to get some more clothes and things. Unless you want to go and get some rest?"

Lucy shakes her head no.

I'm not leaving this room without Drew.

"I didn't think you would. Will you be okay for a while?"

"Yeah, I'll text you a list of some things I forgot to grab. I need my work bag from my car too."

"Sounds good." He stoops down and kisses the top of Drew's head. "I'll see you soon, buddy. Do you want me to grab you some more toys?"

"Yeah! I want my big blocks and dine-saurs."

"Okay."

"And a stuffie!"

"You got it, bud." He kisses Lucy and then thanks Bree for coming before heading out the door.

Bree and Lucy chat for a few more minutes. Drew continues playing until his eyes become heavy. He lays back on the pillows, with one Transformer clutched in each hand.

"I should go so you guys can rest."

"Thanks so much for coming by."

They say their goodbyes. Bree kisses Drew's forehead and then walks through the doorway, waving to them before turning down the hall.

"Do you want to watch a show, buddy?"

"Yeah."

Lucy turns on the TV and finds a cartoon. Drew fights to keep his eyes open. Soon he is fast asleep. A Transformer falls out of his hand. Lucy places both figures on the nightstand by his bed, ready for when he wakes up. She sits down in the recliner beside him, fighting to keep her eyes open.

Eventually, she loses and falls asleep.

Eloise

"Welcome back!" Pam says to her brightly.

"Thanks." Eloise hears the worry in her own voice.

"Let's hope Baby cooperates more this time, huh?"

Eloise follows Pam into the same room as last time. Pam has her lift her shirt and she squirts the gel on her belly. She moves the wand around and clicks on the computer.

After several minutes, Pam finally says, "This is better today. She's being much more helpful."

Eloise's shoulders relax some. Pam continues to make small talk and Eloise answers briefly for the next few minutes.

"I think we have what we need this time. I'll send these over to your doctor and you should hear from him soon."

Eloise looks at Pam closely to gauge her reaction to the scan. She notes her easy smile and calm demeanor.

Good, it must be good.

"Do you want one last look at your daughter?"

"Yes, please."

Pam adjusts the wand until her daughter's blurry profile appears on the screen. She turns it slightly so Eloise can see it better.

"There she is."

Eloise smiles and feels the smallest bit of relief.

"Do you have any names picked out?"

"No, not yet."

"You have some time. I'm sure you'll find the perfect name for her.

Sometimes you don't know until you see them, too."

Eloise repositions her clothing, says goodbye to Pam and heads to her car.

She passes the hardware store on her way home and her thoughts drift to her interaction with Brian. She smiles as she remembers the kindness he showed her.

When she drives by the pottery studio, she notices the sign is still up. She feels her mood lift as she scans the art pieces displayed in the window. Her daughter kicks several times in what Eloise interprets as excitement.

Okay, Baby Girl. I get it.

Eloise slows down and pulls into a parking space. She dials the number on the sign.

"Hello, CB Pottery." A friendly female voice answers.

"Hi, I see that you're hiring."

"Yes, we are. Are you interested?"

"I think I am, yes."

"Great!"

The woman gives her a brief job description.

This sounds great.

Eloise agrees to send her resume, and they set a date and time for an interview. She hangs up the phone and as she backs up the car, she glimpses her face in the rear view mirror. It's impossible for her to miss the happiness reflecting at her.

Lucy

The curtains in the hospital room are closed, blocking out some of the city lights. Drew is sleeping peacefully. Throughout the day, the doctor weaned him off the oxygen mask and now the hospital staff are monitoring him for a few more hours. The doctor said that as long as he continues to improve, they should be able to go home in the morning. Lucy marvels at how small her son looks in the enormous bed.

Allen yawns next to her.

Lucy says to him, "You may as well go home and get some rest. We aren't going anywhere, and I can stay here tonight."

Allen approaches her and rubs her shoulders. "Are you sure, Luce? I know you're tired and that recliner is hardly comfortable for sleeping, especially for you right now."

He shifts his hand to rest it on her belly. Their daughter kicks in response. Allen snorts affectionately.

"I don't want to leave him. I'm okay," Lucy says. "Besides, I need to finish grading those exams."

Allen smiles at her tiredly. "If we're still here tomorrow, will you at least consider going home to sleep for a bit?"

"Yes. I hope we'll get to leave tomorrow, though." She hugs Allen tightly. "Drive safe, okay?"

He lingers a moment as he holds her close. His lips find hers, and he kisses her softly. His hands slide up past her shoulders to gently hold the back of her head. He pulls away to look her in the eyes.

"I love you," he says.

She smiles tiredly. "I love you too."

"Everything is going to be okay," Allen reminds her. He gives her one last hug before leaving.

Lucy opens her laptop and places it on the small table by the window. She turns on the bathroom light and cracks the door so she can see enough to work. She sits in the hard pleather chair and uses the second one as a makeshift desk.

Besides the rustling of her papers, the only noises are the HVAC's occasional humming and nurses bustling quietly through the hallways. Every few pages she glances at Drew, but he's sleeping peacefully each time.

He's fine. He's going to be okay.

Lucy feels her own eyes grow heavy. She finishes the last test and puts everything back in the bag. She turns the room's lights off, but leaves the bathroom one on for when the nurses come to check on them later. She crawls into the bed with Drew, wrapping her arms around him and snuggling him close. Lucy hears his breathing grow deeper and soon her breaths match his.

* * *

"Are you excited to be home, buddy?" Lucy asks Drew the next morning as they pull into the driveway.

"Yeah, I get to see my toys and my room and my stuffies."

Lucy exits the car and unbuckles Drew from his car seat. Even though he's congested and is still coughing quite a bit, his breathing has improved significantly.

Allen catches up with them at the door, carrying their bags.

Lucy steps inside and breathes a sigh of relief.

She immediately wrinkles her nose. "Why do I smell paint?"

"I couldn't sleep last night."

"So you painted? What did you paint?"

"The baby's room."

Lucy stares at him blankly for several seconds. "You painted the baby's room last night?"

"Yeah, want to see it?"

"Of course I do."

Drew has already run off to check on his toys. Lucy and Allen walk down the hallway to the bedrooms. As Allen opens the door, a blast of cold air hits her. "I opened the window to help air it out. Obviously, it didn't help enough, you bloodhound."

Lucy gazes at the walls, the cool gray replaced with a soft blush.

"Thank you," she says to Allen as he loops his arm around her shoulders. "It's perfect. Do you know what it needs next?"

"A plant?"

"Yup. You're basically a mind reader." Lucy smiles and lays her head on Allen's shoulder.

Eloise

A few days after her second ultrasound, Eloise walks into the pottery studio. She marvels at the artwork displays as she walks toward a reception desk at the back. Her footsteps echo on the paint-stained cement floor. A middle-aged woman with brown hair and stylish purple glasses greets her warmly.

"Hi, are you here for the job interview?"

"Yes, I'm Eloise."

"So nice to meet you, Eloise. I'm Jenna. We can go into the office here."

Eloise follows Jenna into a bright room. Artwork hangs from the walls, and pottery pieces decorate the room. Sitting on a bookshelf is a blackbird sculpture.

Of course that's there.

It couldn't be a mallard or something.

"So, Eloise. Tell me a little about yourself. How about we start with what interested you in this job?"

"Okay. Well... I've always loved art, especially drawing, even as a child. But then I grew up and let it slip aside. I think I'd like to pursue it somehow though."

"Great! One perk of working here is that we allow our employees to take our classes and pay just the supply cost."

"Wow! That would be awesome!"

"Yeah, we offer several pottery options and then occasionally we'll have a local artist host a class with their preferred medium."

"Neat!"

"Let me tell you a little about the job. It's mostly scheduling for classes

140

and ordering supplies for the studio. We'll teach you how to set up for the classes and clean up, so that you can help with that too. Does that sound like something you'd be interested in?"

"Definitely."

"Great, I looked over your resume and it seems like your experience could be really helpful here and would be a nice fit for this job. Do you have any questions for me?"

Eloise pauses, thinking about what this change would mean for her life right now. She feels fear and anxiety rise, masking some of her joy. She sees the blackbird sculpture again from the corner of her eye.

"Yes, um. Could we discuss the pay?"

Jenna responds and the number is less than Eloise was hoping to hear.

That's a lot less than I make now. Can I ask for more money?

Unsure though, she says, "Okay."

"I don't want to assume anything…" Jenna glances at her and Eloise sees her eyes rest briefly on her stomach before making eye contact again. "There is the option of bringing children to work here."

"Oh!" Relief relaxes her features. "That would save me so much on daycare expenses."

"Parenting is hard enough, so we try to be as family-friendly as we can." Jenna smiles warmly and asks, "When are you due?"

"October."

"Is this your first?"

"Yes." Eloise looks down and rubs her stomach lightly.

"That's so exciting," she says kindly, and Eloise believes she means it. "I think that about wraps it up. I'll give your references a call, and I'll be in contact in a few days."

"Great! I'm looking forward to it. Thank you for meeting with me."

Eloise leaves the building with a smile again fixed on her face. Her daughter kicks excitedly.

* * *

141

At dinner that night, Eloise picks up a piece of chicken and chews it slowly. She stares at her plate before speaking hesitantly.

Just say it and get it over with.

Plus, he's in a good mood today.

"I interviewed for a job today."

"You what?" Parker's fork stops halfway to his mouth as he looks at her like she lost her mind.

"I interviewed for a job."

"Where? What's wrong with your job?"

"Nothing. I just thought it might be nice to try something different. It's at the pottery studio."

"The pottery studio? Why? There's no way that pays as much as your job now does."

"It doesn't, but they'll…"

Parker interrupts her before she can finish the sentence. "God, Eloise. Are you trying to ruin your life? First getting pregnant and now this?"

She avoids the urge to roll her eyes.

Like I'm the only reason I got pregnant.

"I just thought it might be a nice change for me, and they'll let me bring the baby to work."

Parker stays silent for a minute.

Has he even considered that we'll need to find a daycare and how much it costs?

She knows the answer.

Eloise looks at him sitting across from her. Deep stress lines mark his forehead and his eyes look tired.

What's he thinking?

The level of disconnect in their relationship slams into her chest like a freight train.

She tries a different, softer approach. "What do you think I should do about the job?"

"I don't know what there is to think about. We can't afford for you to make less."

Sure, now it's "we."

Seeing that some of the anger has left his features though, she quietly says, "If you don't think I should accept the job if they offer it, I won't."

She feels her daughter give one long, hard kick.

"But at some point, you have to accept that we're having a baby. Together."

Parker briefly meets her eyes but doesn't reply.

They finish their meal in silence. Eloise swallows past the lump in her throat and is thankful when Parker gets up from the table, even if he leaves his dishes for her to put away.

Lucy

Their local greenhouse is surprisingly quiet for a Saturday. Lucy reminds
herself that it is nearing the end of its brief busy season. Now that Drew is
better, she's finally getting her annual Mother's Day gift- picking out their
summer plants as a family. It's a day she always looks forward to, and today
she breathes in the quiet and gazes at the lush colors around her. She looks at
Drew running between the aisles, his color bright, and she sighs with gratitude.
She moves to stand beside him at a table overflowing with petunias.

"Do you like the red or purple flowers, Drew?"

"Red!"

"Okay." Lucy adds two to their cart and she grabs two of the dark, almost
black, purple, too.

They continue to stroll through the aisles, picking out zinnias, begonias,
geraniums, dahlias, a new peony bush to remind her of her grandma.... By
the time they are done, their cart is a forest of greens, reds, purples, pinks
and white and there isn't room for a single more plant.

"Sucalants!" Drew points and yells at a tiered display of succulents waiting
near the checkout.

Lucy gently touches Allen's arm as they approach it. "Stop here for a second."

"We don't have room for any more!"

"Oh hush. Are you going to deny your son the joy of a new plant?" She
nods at Drew's glowing face and winks at Allen.

He rolls his eyes and shakes his head. "What plant do you want this year,
buddy?" he asks.

Drew looks at all the succulents carefully before grabbing one with thick light green leaves. He shows it to Lucy, a wide smile on his face as he touches the leaves gently.

"It soft!"

"Yeah, it is soft. Great choice. I love that one."

"Can I put it in my turtle pot?!"

"Of course. I think it should fit perfectly in there."

At home, Allen and Lucy unload the flowers from the car while Drew rides his tricycle around the driveway.

"Let's just set these on the porch steps. I'll plant them later this week. I'm feeling kind of tired."

"Yeah, you probably are after picking all these out..." Allen grumbles. Lucy ignores him, knowing he isn't really serious.

"I should probably plant his succulent today, though."

Lucy goes to the garage to find the tortoise planter that she bought at a garage sale fifteen years ago. She tries to remember all the plants it's held and can't.

That's a lot of dead plants...

It's been awhile since I've killed one, though.

She's thankful that her therapist at the time suggested this hobby as a relaxation strategy and loves that she's able to include her son in it now, too.

The turtle sat on a shelf collecting dust until Drew found it last year and insisted that they put a plant in it. She puts a few small stones in the bottom before taking it to her gardening table.

"Drew!" She steps into the garage doorway. "Do you want to help me plant your succulent?"

"Yeah!" He hops off the tricycle. It topples over and he leaves it laying on its side as he runs to meet her.

"Okay, let's get the shovel and dirt."

Drew climbs onto the stool that sits in front of her workbench. He pets the turtle's head.

Lucy brings the dirt over and puts some on the shovel.

"Okay, put a little dirt in the bottom there."

She helps guide Drew's hands as they pour the dirt into the planter.

"Whoopsie!" Drew says as some spills over the sides. He glances at her to check her reaction. She smiles down at him warmly while guilt wraps around her heart.

I hate that he had to question my response...

But you're trying, lady. And that counts for a lot.

"That's okay. It's okay to get a little messy when we work with plants."

"Yeah, it okay." Drew beams back at her.

"Okay, now let's take your plant out. We have to be careful."

Lucy tips the plant over on its side slightly. "Let's just shake it a little to loosen it."

Drew's hands reach out to help and he shakes the plant violently. The leaves flail like it's in a tropical storm.

"Whoa! Gentle, buddy! We don't want to break it."

He shakes it lighter and looks at Lucy. "Like this?"

"Much better." She carefully puts her finger between the dirt and the plastic pot to help release it. It slides out slowly and drops lightly onto the table.

"There we go. Now let's carefully put it into your turtle."

She hands the plant to Drew and helps him center it in the planter.

"Perfect. We just need to add a little dirt on top."

Drew enthusiastically grabs a handful of dirt.

"Now what?" He looks at Lucy with bright eyes.

"Now just put it around the plant like this." Lucy puts her handful around the succulent, tucking it in. Drew copies her on the other side.

"Looks great, buddy. I think we're all done. Do you want to put it on the porch?"

"Yeah!"

Drew jumps off the stool and races to the porch. "I want it right there!" He points to the top step while Lucy follows behind him with the plant.

"That's the perfect spot."

Drew goes to the turtle, pets its head one more time, and then runs back to his tricycle. Allen sits on the steps where he's been watching them, his knees pulled up, chin resting on one hand and a small smile touching his lips.

Lucy looks at him pointedly.

"And you gave me s-h-i-t about buying another plant." She clucks her tongue and shakes her head as she puts the potting materials away.

Eloise

June

Eloise answers her phone quickly when she recognizes the studio's number. Her stomach feels heavy, but not because of the baby.

"Hello, Eloise?"

"Yes, this is Eloise."

"Hi! This is Jenna from CB Pottery. How are you?"

"I'm alright. How are you?"

"Fantastic. I called your references, and as I expected they gave glowing reviews. I'd like to formally offer you the position."

Her throat burns and she fights the tears forming in her eyes, willing them to stay contained.

"Eloise? Are you still there?"

"Yes…" Her voice wavers and Eloise swallows past the pain. "I'm sorry…I can't accept the job."

Now there's a pause on the other end of the line. Jenna finally responds.

"Okay, I'm really sorry to hear that." She hears the sincerity in Jenna's voice. "If anything changes please call back."

"I will. Thank you."

She ends the call as tears fall quickly down her cheeks. Eloise's breath hitches and a sob escapes. She covers her mouth and then furiously wipes her eyes. Her baby kicks once again.

"I know. I'm disappointed too." Her voice breaks.

If this helps our relationship, it's worth it though…

Two kicks this time as her eyes fill again. She sets the phone on the table. Eloise turns away, but then through the tears, she sees the blurry outline of the paint cans still sitting by the front door, a light layer of dust covering the lids. She realizes she's going to wait forever for Parker to paint the room.

She wipes her eyes again and picks her phone back up to call her mom.

"Hey, hun!"

"Hi, mom. How are you?"

"Fine. How are you today?"

"Also fine. Hey, would you be able to help me paint the baby's room next weekend?"

"Oh...What day were you thinking?"

"It doesn't matter. Saturday?"

"Well, I usually grocery shop on Saturdays..."

"Okay, how about Sunday?"

"Well, Monday is going to be a busy day at work, and I don't want to get home too late..."

Eloise expected her mom to make excuses, but she sighs, anyway.

I should have known better than to ask for help on such short notice.

Or at all.

How silly of me to assume a parent would want to be there for their child?

"How about Dad? Can he help?"

"I can ask him, but he hurt his back last week, so I'm not sure he'll be able to. The idiot drank too much at the bar and fell off a stool."

"Okay, never mind then."

"Sorry," the insincerity is clear.

"It's fine." *It isn't.* "I have to go."

"Okay, love you."

"Love you too."

She hangs up quickly before her mom can hear her next sob.

If my sister called her, I bet she'd drop everything though.

She takes in another difficult, shaky breath and breathes out through her mouth.

She walks to the bathroom to splash cold water on her face and eyes. She uses a tissue, allowing her to breathe more clearly. Before she turns off the bathroom light, she glimpses her face.

There's no time for sadness.

Eloise returns to the living room. She carefully picks up one of the paint cans and takes it to the second bedroom. When she stands up, she feels a cramp run briefly through her pelvis.

After it ends, she comes back for the other can. She hesitates, though.

Should I lift another one?

Who else will do it?

She picks it up, with no cramping this time, and then finds some paint-brushes, tape and a drop cloth. Thankfully, the room is already white, so she doesn't have to prime it. She turns on some music, spreads the drop cloth on the floor, and starts taping the trim.

Her phone rings again, interrupting her music. She lets it go to voicemail. A few minutes later, she sees a text message appear on her phone. It's Sarah. She gets to the end of the wall and rips off the tape before picking up her phone to call Sarah back.

"Hey! I wondered if you wanted to get some coffee or lunch. What are you up to?"

"Getting ready to paint the nursery."

"Is Parker painting it?"

"No."

"...is anyone else there helping?"

Eloise sighs before saying, "No."

"I'll be right there."

"You don't have to."

"I'm not doing anything, and you shouldn't be painting a room by yourself while pregnant."

"Fine. I'll finish taping the trim at least."

"Okay, I'll be there in about 15 minutes. And Eloise, don't you dare use a stepladder to tape up the ceiling."

"Oh...um, too late."

"Eloise!"

"Just kidding." She smirks into the phone. "Thanks, Sarah. See you soon."

* * *

"I love this color."

A few hours later, Eloise and Sarah are standing in the nursery admiring Sarah's work.

"Me too. It reminds me of my grandma's garden. I didn't notice it at the store, but that's all I can think about now." Eloise smiles brightly at the walls and then looks at her friend. "Thanks so much for helping today, Sarah. I really appreciate it."

"No worries. I'm happy to help."

"Do you want to get some dinner? I'll pay as a thank you."

"Sure! Where do you want to go?" Sarah asks as she follows Eloise down the hallway.

"I've had a craving for pasta the last few days…"

"Italian it is!"

Before they can leave, Eloise hears Parker's key in the lock.

Shit. What kind of mood will he be in today?

Sarah turns as the door opens. She smiles in greeting, but Eloise sees it looks less genuine than usual.

"Hi, Parker," Sarah says as he enters the room.

"Hi…." Eloise can tell he doesn't remember Sarah's name, even though he's met her several times.

"Sarah came to help paint," she offers in what she hopes he perceives as helping.

"Gotcha." Parker walks to the fridge and takes out a beer.

"We were just about to get some dinner," Sarah says while looking at Eloise. Before either can invite him, Parker pops the lid.

"I ate with the guys. Have fun though." Parker smiles, *grimaces really*, at them.

He sits down in front of the TV. Sarah watches him before glancing at Eloise.

Eloise shakes her head slightly. They silently put on their shoes. Eloise says a quick goodbye and then pulls the door closed quietly behind her.

"Do you want me to drive?" Sarah asks softly.

"Sure."

They buckle up. The car is quiet for a few minutes. Sarah finally takes a deep breath.

"Eloise, I'm only going to say one thing. You deserve more in life." Her eyes don't leave the road. It wouldn't have mattered because Eloise stares out the passenger window, avoiding any confrontation. "That's it. Now let's have a fun dinner."

Eloise finally looks at Sarah. Sarah smiles contagiously at her, and it radiates empathy.

"Deal." Eloise smiles back at her.

Lucy

Lucy unlocks her office door. Her bag slips off her shoulder, and she spills her coffee slightly as she reaches to catch it.

"Dammit," she whispers quietly.

As Lucy walks around her desk, trying to brush off the coffee that has spilled on her shirt, she looks out the window to check the nest as she does every time she comes to her office. The mama bird finished it several weeks ago, and Lucy has been waiting not so patiently for it to be filled.

"Oh!" she says loudly with surprise. Nestled inside today are three bluish green eggs, speckled with brown spots.

"What's going on, Lucy? Are you okay?"

She turns back to the door and sees Angela standing there.

"Yes, check this out!" She points out the window. "A mother blackbird built a nest outside my window, and I've been watching for eggs the last several weeks. And today there are some in it!"

Angela joins her at the window to look too.

"So sweet."

"I know. This is the first year she's done that. You know what else is crazy? *Blackbird* is my favorite song."

Angela beams at her. "I love animal spirit guides. I'll send you some info on the blackbird totem."

"I'd be interested in reading that. Thanks!"

"I may have to stop in more often so that I can check out your friends."

"Come by anytime."

* * *

A few days later, while Lucy is finishing packing up her office for summer break, Angela knocks on her door.

"Hey! How are your spirit guides today?"

Lucy glances out the window to see the blackbird sitting on her nest. "Looking good I think. Three eggs still and the mama has been very dutiful."

"Good." Angela holds out a small bag. "I have something for you."

"What is it?" Lucy takes the bag, tissue paper crinkling as she removes it. Resting gently inside the paper is a light blue mug with hand painted tree branches stretching across it. Sitting on a branch is a blackbird, painted so that looks like it is calling out.

"Oh my goodness, Angela. It's beautiful."

"I saw it at the farmer's market and immediately thought of you."

She reaches out to hug Angela. "Thank you. It's my new favorite mug."

Eloise

Eloise sits in the doctor's office, again, staring at the cheap hotel art on the walls.

Two quick knocks sound on the door.

"Hello. How are you today?"

Her OB GYN comes in wheeling his ancient computer cart.

"Good. How are you?"

"Superb. Thanks for asking. How are you and baby? Have you had any more unusual experiences?"

That's a strange way to phrase it...

Eloise answers with some relief, "No. Now that you mention it, I haven't."

"Good. Your ultrasound looked okay, nothing seriously concerning."

Eloise considers these words. "Was there something mildly concerning?"

Dr. Sattler hesitates. "No. Not really. We still didn't get the best shot of her heart, but I think it looked okay." He looks at Eloise's tight face and his eyes and tone soften a little. "I don't think you should worry. Any bleeding or cramping?"

"Some cramping still."

"How often is that happening now?"

"Um… maybe once a week or so."

Or maybe a few times a week....

"How long do they last?"

"Just a few seconds."

"Try drinking a glass of water when that happens, okay? You may just be dehydrated."

Back to dehydration. I'm going to have to get one of those water backpacks hikers use and wear it around all day.

"Okay, I can do that."

The doctor takes his usual measurements, and they listen to her baby's heart again. Dr. Sattler removes the monitor and turns around.

"Starting this week, I want you to keep track of your baby's kicks." He hands her a card. Eloise looks down at it and sees a series of tiny boxes.

"Once a day, I want you to pay attention to baby's movements. You should feel ten kicks in an hour. When you do, check this little box here and bring this card back to every appointment."

"Okay, sounds good."

Dr. Sattler hands her a lab order. "It's also time for your glucose screening test. Have you done one before?"

"No."

"Pick a time in the next week or two to go to the lab. You don't have to worry about fasting for this one. They'll give you a sugary drink, have you wait an hour and then draw your blood. As long as the results come back okay you won't have to do the three-hour test."

Eloise's eyes widen. "Let's hope not. That sounds terrible."

"I'll be honest, it isn't fun." He stands up. "As long as you don't have more questions, I'll see you in a couple of weeks."

Eloise looks at her calendar before leaving the room, flagging a day after work for a lab appointment.

I don't want to take more days off if I can help it...

Later that night when she's resting on the couch, her feet on Parker's legs, she notices the baby moving. She glances at the clock and starts counting in her head.

One kick.

A few minutes pass.

Two.

Parker laughs at the show he has on.

Three.

The episode finishes and the next one starts. Several minutes have passed without additional kicks. Eloise shifts slightly to see if the baby will move.

Nothing.

She shifts more.

"What are you doing? Why are you moving so much?" Parker asks impatiently.

"Nothing. Just uncomfortable."

Four.

Thank goodness.

The hour passes with five kicks. She goes to bed, slightly concerned.

Maybe she's just sleeping...

Lucy

A large maple shades the backyard, and sunlight dapples the ground through its leafy branches. Lucy sits on the back steps drinking her coffee while Drew plays in the grass. She's using the blackbird mug Angela gave her this week.

"Mom! Look I found!"

"What is it, buddy?"

Drew races up to her, and she holds out her hand. He places a dead stink bug in her palm.

"Gross!" She immediately drops it.

"It bug!" Drew laughs hysterically before running away to find something else.

Lucy shakes her head and kicks the dead bug away.

Allen comes out onto the porch, freshly showered. Lucy stands up and walks toward him to be enveloped in his embrace.

"I was just thinking it would be nice to have a patio out here. Update the space somehow, so it's a little more fun for the kids to play." Lucy ends half under her breath with, "Maybe add a little garden shed for me..."

"Sounds like a lot of money," Allen says seriously.

"I know," Lucy sighs. "Maybe someday. A girl can dream. I need to get to my gardening club."

"I still can't believe you like hanging out with ninety-year-old women in your free time."

"They're not ninety. Well... Janet may be." Lucy looks thoughtful and then her eyes brighten as she says, "I love those women, though. They're so sweet. It's like being with my grandma. Plus, John is there, so it isn't just women!"

"I know. Have fun, hun." He kisses her cheek.

Lucy turns to walk inside but stops as she enters the doorway.

"Hey Drew, I think your dad wants to see one of your surprises too!" She closes the screen door and laughs when she hears Allen say, "Oh… Thanks, buddy…"

Fifteen minutes later, Lucy pulls into the gravel lot of a nearby park. She sees Margaret, Janet, and John standing inside the pavilion. The sight of them warms her heart. As she approaches them, Margaret says, "Oh, Lucy. You are just so cute. How are you feeling, dear?"

"Pretty good. Tired, but good."

"And how is the family? How's Drew?"

"He's great. I left them outside where he was playing with dead stink bugs."

The group laughs. They love hearing stories about Drew. John leaves to finish gathering the supplies while the women continue to talk.

"Will I be seeing you at our book club next week?" Margaret asks Lucy. "I really enjoyed this month's book. I thought–"

John walks toward them then and claps his hands together once excitedly, interrupting their conversation. "Betty and Gina won't be joining us. They're visiting their daughter this week and Sue was touring a retirement village today. I think it's just us then, so we may as well get started." He finishes his directive with a thumbs up.

Veteran Army General, but good-natured John marches off to start work. Lucy and Margaret take their supplies and walk towards the flowerbeds lining the park's perimeter.

"Lucy, I thought you wouldn't want to bend down to weed, so why don't you start with weeding the planters and then you can water the plants?"

"Oh Margaret, that's sweet of you, but you don't have to do that!"

"I want to, dear." She pats Lucy's back affectionately. "I keep forgetting to tell you- I'm going to drop off a couple frozen meals for you too for when the baby comes. I was thinking chicken pot pie and maybe meatballs unless you don't want those." She pulls on her gardening gloves. "I'll wait until closer to your due date though, so you don't have to store them long."

"Margaret, you are just the sweetest. Thank you."

"Oh nonsense. I love taking care of the people I love." She smiles at Lucy and slowly walks to the brightly colored flower beds.

Lucy turns away to weed the planters, wiping her eyes quickly before putting her dirt-covered gloves on.

In the few years I've known her, Margaret has told me she loves me more than my mom ever did.

Eloise

A knock sounds on her front door and when Eloise answers it, her dad is on the other side holding a toolbox.

"Dad! What are you doing here?"

Her dad holds up the toolbox. "I thought I'd come help you with that closet door in the spare room."

Eloise had forgotten about it but is immediately touched by her dad's thoughtfulness.

"Oh, thanks Dad!"

"Hey, Parker." Her dad nods at Parker sitting on the couch.

He takes his shoes off and starts walking down the hall. Eloise follows him and when she gets to the room, he already has tools spread on the floor and is attempting to fix the sliding closet door that has fallen off the track.

Eloise watches him work quietly for a minute, as usual unsure of what to say to him.

While not entirely foreign, her dad's presence is something still not familiar to her. Growing up, his moods constantly shifted, and his temper always came quickly. Once she and her sister left home and became adults, Eloise noticed that her dad's moods seemed to improve, too. She's thought about this a lot lately as motherhood approaches. Maybe the stress of parenting was too much, or maybe he just reached an age where his personality suddenly changed. She doesn't really know the reason, but she's thankful for whatever caused the change.

He still visits the bar more often than she would like, and they don't talk regularly. There is always a feeling of awkwardness whenever they are alone together, both unsure what a father-daughter relationship should even look like. Being with him doesn't automatically stress her out anymore, though.

That's an improvement, at least.

She realizes he's breathing heavily and sweating, more than she would expect for the task he's doing.

"Are you feeling okay, Dad?" Eloise asks with concern.

"Yup, just getting old I guess," he smiles at her, but she remains unconvinced.

"How's your back feeling?"

"Fine?" he says with confusion in his tone.

"Mom said you hurt it."

"Nope. Beats me."

She wanted to help me so little that she lied?

Feeling hurt, but recognizing her dad had nothing to do with it, she changes the subject instead.

"What's she up to today? Why didn't she come too?"

"Oh, she was cleaning when I left. I didn't tell her I was coming. I needed a break from her nagging."

Eloise laughs. "So you just walked out the door and assumed she wouldn't notice?"

"She'll notice sometime. I haven't heard from her yet." He pats his pockets. "But actually, I think I left my phone in the car..."

He shrugs indifferently and Eloise chuckles.

Her dad adjusts the door one last time, and it clicks back into the track.

"There it goes. Perfect."

"Thanks, Dad. Hey, can you look at the front door jamb too?"

"Sure thing."

She leaves the room while her dad packs up his tools.

She hears him walk towards the front room and Parker asks him, "All set?"

"Yup, good as new."

"Want a beer?"

"Sure. Let me take a gander at this jamb too."

Eloise walks into the kitchen and Parker yells to her, "Hey Eloise, can you get your dad a beer?"

She brings one out and hands it to her dad.

He smiles at her as he takes the can.

"Thanks."

He opens the front door, letting a draft of cold air in. Within ten minutes, he has the jamb back to normal. He packs up his things, grabs his beer and joins Parker on the couch.

"Can I get you guys some snacks?" Eloise asks.

"Yeah, babe," Parker says as he continues to watch the TV screen.

Eloise stands in the kitchen and watches them quietly for a second. She shifts from one foot to the other and realizes she doesn't really know how to be comfortable around either of them. Before she can consider this further, her vision flickers again, and this time she's standing in an office she's never seen before. She walks around a desk to look out the window beside it. Outside she sees sidewalks crisscrossing a lawn and a large tree. On one branch sits a nest and inside are three speckled eggs. Eloise continues to watch as one egg shifts slightly. She gasps as she realizes the egg is hatching. She sees a tiny beak push through the shell, followed by the top of a wet head. Eloise sees a black blur in the corner of her eye and realizes the mother blackbird has returned to the nest. The bird stretches her wings wide, and all Eloise sees is black.

She blinks then and sees her dining room rug and her dad's concerned face over hers. She's laying on the floor face up but has no memory of falling.

"Are you okay?" Her dad asks her. She does a quick mental check and nothing hurts, yet.

"Yeah, I think so."

"Has this happened before? Have you talked to your doctor about it?" he asks while helping her up.

"Yes, not quite like this, though. He thought maybe I was dehydrated. I should drink some water."

"I'll get you some. You should sit down."

"Thanks, Dad."

Eloise knows she should feel comforted at his concern, but she can't help still feeling uncomfortable. It feels so foreign to her.

How is this the same parent who was either yelling at me or ignoring me when I was a kid?

He hands her a glass, and she takes a long drink.

And what is with the blackbird?

Lucy

Lucy took a break from teaching summer classes this year, so she could spend more one on one time with Drew before the baby comes. She's taken him on several "special adventures" so far. Sometimes they've been planned and sometimes not.

The unplanned ones have been some of the best.

We've had a lot of fun during all of them though, mostly. Just a few hiccups.

Planting flowers with her gardening club.

Making new friends at the library's Story Time.

The children's museum where he threw a fit when it was time to leave.

People probably thought I was abducting him.

At least I kept my cool.

And the rest of our day was great.

She takes him inside the art studio for today's outing- a toddler/preschool paint class. The room is exactly what you would expect when a bunch of three-to-five-year-olds mix with art supplies, beautiful chaos.

After the teacher provides some initial instructions, they are free to work at their own pace. Lucy helps Drew with his smock and places some paint on the tray for him. She watches him for a minute before starting on her own canvas. She considers what she wants to paint. An image of her grandma's peonies appears in her mind.

Yes, perfect.

She selects a light pink paint and dips her brush into it, visualizing her grandma standing in her garden with the flowers behind her.

Lucy's hand creates long, careful strokes with the brush. Her vision shimmers in the odd but familiar way and she sees a field of flowers, drawn by someone with more skill than she is currently showing.

"Mama, look!"

The vision breaks as she looks at Drew. Paint covers him, but he smiles widely while pointing at his canvas. On it are a few indecipherable but colorful blobs.

"Wow, buddy! Tell me about your painting."

"Well, this is a T-Rex." He points at a green spot with his brush before pointing to a light blue one. "And this is our house."

"I love it. Do you want to add some more stuff to your painting?"

He turns back to his easel. As he brings the brush up to his canvas again a large splotch of paint falls to the floor.

"Oops."

Drew looks to her for reassurance.

"That's okay, buddy. That's why there's a cloth on the floor, to catch any messes."

Drew happily continues his painting.

I'll have to tell my doctor I had another "hallucination."

She sighs deeply.

Maybe there's a different medication I can try that would be safer and work better than last time.

They finish their paintings and clean up their supplies.

After they are done and as she buckles Drew into his car seat, he asks if they can come back sometime. She smiles, happy that he enjoyed their time together.

"Sure, buddy. I had fun with you."

"Can we get ice cream? Please?" He looks at her with dramatically sad, puppy-dog eyes.

Where did he learn to do that to get what he wants?

"We haven't had lunch yet, hun. Let's go home and have lunch and then maybe we can get it later with dad."

She hears him grumble quietly and hangrily, "Are you kiddin' me?"

She chuckles to herself before offering him a package of fruit snacks for the drive.

Eloise

Eloise and Sarah are having a leisurely lunch together. Like every day, the office is slow, and they've run out of work to do.

They've exhausted the usual catching up small talk. A comfortable quiet has fallen between them. Eloise has gotten a little lost in her thoughts.

Her mind has repeatedly gone back to the other day when she fell. It bothers her she has no memory of what happened, and she feels annoyed that the doctor's office hasn't called her back yet.

She sees Sarah shift uncomfortably, looking down at her lunch.

"Has Parker been any more excited about the baby?"

Eloise pauses as Sarah studies her closely.

"Not really," she answers simply. She watches as Sarah opens her mouth. "I know what you're thinking. I can't leave him."

I can't hurt his feelings.

And leaving on top of everything else going on right now seems like too much.

Sarah softly asks, "Why not? You aren't happy with him anymore, El."

Now Eloise looks down. She can't stand seeing the pity and sadness in Sarah's eyes.

"I keep hoping something will change, that things will go back to how they were at first."

And if I leave him, who am I going to find when I have a kid? It's not like the options were great before that.

"But how long are you going to wait?"

She thinks of the kindness her dad showed her after she fell, but then childhood memories of her parents' arguing fill her head. She sees a little girl

168

as if from a balcony view, sitting alone on her bed crying.

Tears fill her own eyes at the distorted memory.

"I don't know yet," she answers quietly as she wipes them away. She feels her daughter push against her ribs.

No matter what happens, I won't let that be you. I promise. I just need to figure some stuff out.

Lucy

Early in the day, Lucy decided she was too tired to take Drew out today.

Giant mistake.

Being cooped up has increased the tension between them, and they have gotten into several toddler-sized arguments. She has had to check herself a few times and walk away for a moment of peace more than once. She's still in the kitchen after Drew jumped on the couch cushions for the tenth time today despite her pulling him off EVERY time and telling him, "Couches are for sitting."

But at least you knew you needed a break and didn't take it out on your kid.

She opens the microwave to take out her now thrice-reheated coffee and starts putting the dried dishes away.

"MOM!"

"Yes, hun?"

"WHERE ARE YOU?!?"

"In the kitchen."

Drew runs into the room holding a stuffed elephant.

"Mom! I want see ef-efant today!"

"Okay, like a picture or video of an elephant?"

"NO!" Drew widens his eyes dramatically. "A *real* one."

"Buddy, elephants don't live here and there aren't any at the zoos by us."

"BUT I WANT SEE EF-EFANT!" Drew stomps his foot. "NOW!"

"Of course."

Because why wouldn't *the Chief Tantrum Officer decide he needs to see an impossible animal today?*

Lucy tries to think of a realistic alternative to offer.

"I'm sorry, bud. We can't see a real elephant today, but maybe we can find a show about elephants."

"NOOOO!"

Drew throws his elephant onto the floor and runs from the room screaming.

You thought you could negotiate with someone who held you emotionally hostage over the wrong color cup yesterday?

She hears toys clattering to the floor in the living room and yells, "If you make a mess, you're going to clean it up."

"NO! I NOT CLEAN IT UP!"

Her simmering anger starts to boil. Lucy closes her eyes and breathes deeply through her nose.

One...

Two...

Three...

Silence.

Suspicious, she peeks out to make sure he's okay. He's lying on the floor, still pouting but no longer furious.

Living with a toddler really is like living with the Incredible Hulk.

She finishes with the dishes and as she comes back to the living room, she steps over the toys scattered *all* over the floor.

She calmly says, "Come help clean up, please."

"No... I can't," Drew says into the carpet. "It's impossible..."

"Drew..." Lucy looks at him sternly.

He continues to lie there, unmoving. She sighs heavily, wishing for the patience of a hundred nuns.

Maybe if I try something new...

"How about if we turn on a song and see if we can finish cleaning everything up before it ends?"

"Fine." He narrows his eyebrows and pouts his lips.

Lucy turns away and rolls her eyes slightly while selecting a song on her phone.

"Alright! Let's go, buddy."

She starts cleaning up and it doesn't take long before he's not only helping but laughing.

Once the room is clean, she feels more at ease.

"Hey mom, what do you call a naked hippo?"

"What?"

"A hippo! AH HA HA! Get it?!?"

Lucy laughs at her son and looks at him fondly. "Good one, buddy."

She takes a deep breath and lets it out slowly.

Remember- the days are long, but the years are short.

Her phone vibrates on the table, and she sees a text message from Emily.

"Kids are driving me nuts. Wine date in the backyard?"

Lucy has never texted back faster.

"Absolutely. I'll bring some mocktails. See you in a few."

Lucy looks at Drew playing with one of his action figures. She takes advantage of this quiet moment to collect her aluminum wine glasses and a couple of bottles from the fridge. As she sets them on the counter she realizes that her son's meltdown didn't trigger any childhood memories.

That's growth, babe!

She smiles proudly and grabs their shoes on her way back into the living room.

"Let's go outside, buddy. Nora's coming to play."

Ten minutes later, Lucy and Emily sit on her back steps, watching their older kids play in the yard. Emily has placed a blanket and toys down for Wesley, but he's since crawled away and is now pulling the grass up blade by blade.

"I'm so glad you texted me. I was going crazy today, too," Lucy says.

"Yeah. I tried gentle parenting, but this kid isn't gentle child-ing today. Or maybe Mercury is in retrograde. I don't know."

Lucy laughs. "Something. I think I just feel cranky today."

"You can blame the pregnancy." Emily winks at her before taking a sip of her drink. "You look great though, glowing as they say."

"Thanks. It's the sweat." Emily laughs at her. "Seriously though, it feels like there's a furnace burning inside me all the time. These hot days don't help."

Lucy wipes moisture from her forehead. Images of their early wine dates drift into her thoughts.

Relaxing on these same steps with Emily in the twilight.

Chatting quietly until the fireflies came out to dance.

"These dates look way different from when we first moved here," Lucy says, watching her son make mud pies with Nora.

I hope the hose is attached so I can spray him off before we go back inside.

"What do you mean?" Emily asks sarcastically. "Didn't Allen crawl around in the grass pantless during one of them like Wes is doing right now?"

Lucy snorts at the image Emily's created.

"I love being a mom and my kids are the most important thing to me..." Lucy watches her son running through the backyard with his friend. "But sometimes I miss my life BC. Before Children."

"Me too. The freedom to do whatever you want whenever you want?"

"Yes! Exactly! To not be needed ALL the time." She sips her drink. "Sometimes I get so overwhelmed by it all, and then I have such little patience with Drew."

"I know, I do the same with Nora."

"And I just get so mad so fast and then feel awful and guilty." Lucy pauses for a second, considering. "Oh my gosh, I feel so guilty BECAUSE I love him so much. I haven't thought of it that way before."

Duh.

HOURS spent in therapy and I'm just now realizing that.

"Yeah. I-"

"Mommmmmm!"

Emily's next thought is cut short with the latest fire to be put out. Both friends sigh and smile at each other sympathetically.

"Man, I can't wait until we can put some Riesling in these cups," Lucy says.

"Cheers to that, my friend."

They clink their cups together before each taking a long sip.

III

Trimester Three

Eloise

July

Eloise and her mom exchange texts for her upcoming baby shower.

I can't believe I only have a few months left before I become a mother...

She feels equal parts panic and excitement.

At least I think that's what I feel...

"What time do you want me to come to the shower?"

"I was planning on getting there a few hours before to set up, so 9 probably."

"You're getting there at 9 or you want me there at 9?"

"Both."

Eloise pauses before she replies. She assumed the mother-to-be was exempt from helping with the baby shower prep. She thinks about telling her mom that, but before she can decide her mom texts again.

"I have your aunt coming to help, and you know she's going to be late. She only offered to plan games and decorations, and I have to do the rest."

"Okay..." She considers what else to say but sees her mom typing back.

"Nevermind... It seems like you don't want to help me so I'll just do it myself... It's fine..."

Eloise feels the typical guilt settle over her. She pictures her mom furiously typing to her as she complains aloud about how unhelpful her daughter is.

Eloise types back, "I'll be there at 9."

She exhales loudly and sets her phone aside.

* * *

When she walks into the rental hall a few days later (at nine), her mom is busy prepping food, and her dad is setting up tables.

"Hi, honey! No Parker?"

"No, when I asked, he said showers were for women."

Her mom laughs. Eloise doesn't.

"What do you need me to do?" Eloise asks.

"You could help your dad with chairs."

She pauses before replying, "I don't really want to lift a bunch of stuff today if I can help it."

Her mom glances at her, and Eloise notes the surprised look on her face. "Okay, that's probably a good idea I suppose. You can get the tablecloths out. It makes more sense to lay them down before the chairs are up anyway."

Her aunt walks in just as the tables and chairs are finished.

"Eloise! How are you, sweetie?" she wraps her in a warm hug. Before Eloise can answer, her mom bustles out of the kitchen.

"Great timing, now we can decorate."

Eloise sprinkles some of the baby-bottle shaped confetti on the tables. She can hear her mom and aunt quietly bickering on the other side of the room and feels the tension increasing in her neck muscles.

It would have been so nice to just show up today and enjoy the party.

Her dad comes over to place a vase of baby's breath on the table. As he walks away, he says, "Seems like just yesterday we brought you home from the hospital."

She looks up in surprise.

Is he reminiscing? About my childhood?

Before she can talk to him more, her mom hands her a box of pink tea light candles to place on the tables.

"We only have twenty minutes before the party starts."

They rush to finish decorating and there's a noticeable sense of friction in the air. Her parents are arguing just as the first guests come through the doors. They stop yelling when they see the door open, and in walk distant cousins Eloise hasn't seen or talked to since the family Christmases held when she was a little girl.

The next few hours pass quickly. Eloise greets guests, helps refill the punch, hands out cake, makes small talk, opens presents, says goodbye to guests... Everyone finally leaves and Eloise breathes a sigh of relief that the day is almost over. She sits down for a minute to rest. She has a headache, and her feet are killing her.

As she's clearing off the tables and putting chairs away, her mom smiles, "That was a nice day."

Eloise smiles back halfheartedly, "Yes. It was."

"You got so many great gifts." She looks at Eloise, her eyes lingering on the fact that she is sitting. She doesn't even need to say anything for Eloise to feel guilty about not helping. Eloise sighs and stands back up to clear off the table she's near.

"We need to vacuum too before we go, Eloise."

Eloise notes the subtle hint and leaves to find the vacuum.

Two hours later she has finally arrived home. She sits on the couch to rest her tired feet. As she lays her head back, she reflects on the shower and realizes that it's already just a blurred memory.

Lucy

Lucy waits in the doctor's office for her biweekly appointment. Black-and-white newborn photos hang from the walls and there are drawings on the ceiling tiles to provide something for patients to look at no matter the angle of their body.

A thoughtful touch.

She checks the time and feels annoyed that the doctor is running behind.

My appointment should have started twenty minutes ago. I only have thirty minutes before my next client.

A knock finally sounds on the door.

"Hi, Lucy." Dr. Burman smiles. "How are you?"

"Fine," Lucy answers, uncharacteristically short.

Dr. Burman glances at her. "I'm sorry I was late. We have a mom with some complications in the hospital and her doctor was calling to consult me."

Guilt replaces Lucy's annoyance.

That poor Mama.

And here I am worrying about the time.

"Oh, I'm sorry to hear that."

"How have you been feeling?"

"I'm okay. I've been cranky lately."

"How are you sleeping?"

Lucy laughs sarcastically. "What's sleep? I'm waking up a lot to go to the bathroom."

"Unfortunately, that's a not so fun part of pregnancy, along with mood changes. Do you feel you're managing it okay?"

"Yeah. I'm hoping maybe my hormones just needed some time to readjust or something."

"That could be. If you decide you need help, there are certain medications I can prescribe that are safe for you and the baby."

"Okay, I'll keep it in mind."

"I have your glucose screening results, and they look great." Dr. Burman puts Lucy's file aside and stands up. "Let's listen to the heartbeat and take some measurements."

They listen to her daughter's heartbeat, which the doctor assures her sounds perfect. When she measures Lucy's abdomen, she does a double take. She clicks her pen to write the numbers in Lucy's chart.

"You're measuring a little big, a few weeks ahead, actually. It could just be the baby's position today. We'll watch your numbers."

I don't want to birth a toddler.

Dr. Burman takes out a card from the folder, glances at it, and hands it back to Lucy. "Your kick card looks great, too. Seems like Baby is moving well."

"She doesn't seem as busy as Drew was."

"All babies and pregnancies are different. I'm not worried looking at this." Dr. Burman stands to leave. "Any plans this weekend?"

"Nothing too exciting. My sister invited us over, so we'll spend some time with her family."

"I hope you have a great time. Anything else for me today?"

"I don't think so. Just pray I don't have a ten-pound monster baby."

She doesn't remember until she's driving that she forgot to tell the doctor about her visions.

I'll do it next time.

If it happens again.

Eloise

Eloise nervously hands her kick card to Dr. Sattler. The card is slightly moist from her sweaty hands. At her last appointment, the doctor had frowned while looking at the card and told her to keep a close eye on the baby's movements. Since then, she's had an eagle eye for any she felt.

Today he stares at the nearly empty grid before looking at her, concern apparent in his eyes.

"You've been doing this every day?"

Eloise nods.

"Okay, between the fall you had a few weeks ago and the fact that the baby isn't moving as much as we'd like, I think we should hook you up to our monitor to see if we can track some more movements."

Shit.

"What does it mean if the baby isn't moving enough?"

"It could just be the position she's in right now and that you aren't able to feel her well. The monitor will tell us a little more, though."

A few minutes later, Eloise sits in a leather armchair, a band around her stomach. She watches the screen bounce and occasionally feels her daughter move.

Fifteen minutes later, the nurse returns, looks at the sheet and wrinkles her eyebrows.

"I'm going to get you some juice. We'll see if that wakes her up a little."

Panic rises in Eloise's stomach. She downs the apple juice the nurse hands her and offers a silent plea for her baby to get moving.

Please be okay.

Five minutes later the nurse comes back to check the sheet.

"That's a little better. Let's watch for a few more minutes."

This time, she stands in the room for a minute and watches the monitor.

Move, please.

Come on...

"There's a big kick!"

Eloise breathes a sigh of relief.

"Okay, I think that's good. It's a little fewer movements than we would like, but it's good to see Baby moving. We'll probably hook you up to this again at your next appointment just to keep track."

She finishes unstrapping Eloise and looks her in the eye kindly, but seriously.

"Let us know if anything comes up, okay?"

"I will. Thank you."

Lucy

Allen carries Drew up the walkway towards her sister's house with Lucy following closely behind. She's still testy today and has already snapped at, and then apologized to, Allen twice. She knows something is bothering her, but she can't put her finger on what it is.

I wish I could at least stop being such a B.

When they reach the door, Allen knocks three times before opening it unusually slowly.

Oh, my gosh. Just open the damn door, man.

"Surprise!"

Lucy's eyes widen as she walks into Bree's living room. Hanging inside are brightly colored streamers and balloons. A mass of people wait expectantly, and it takes her a second to recognize all of them: Emily holding her baby, Margaret and a couple of her other gardening club members, and her sister and her family, of course. A giant banner hangs from the archway, with a pink donut and the phrase "Sprinkled with love." Gold balloons frame the banner.

"What is this?" Lucy asks.

"A baby sprinkle!"

Lucy looks behind Bree and sees a table overflowing with gifts and another table filled with treats.

"You guys!" Lucy says with misty eyes. She turns to Allen. "You knew about this?"

She affectionately and lightly hits him. He shrugs nonchalantly.

"Come on in and have some snacks! Drew, the kids are playing upstairs. Do you want to go up?"

"Yeah!" Drew climbs up the stairs, tripping halfway but continuing on as if nothing happened. Bree turns back to face Lucy.

"Don't worry, I have the baby monitor on, and Liam is upstairs with them."

Lucy and Allen chat with the guests while people graze at the food table. After a few minutes, she sees Margaret whisper to Bree, who nods her head. Bree takes a bag from the pile of gifts and brings it over to Lucy.

"Lucy, Margaret can't stay long. Do you mind opening her gift?"

"Sorry I can't stay, Lucy. I have to go to my great grandson's soccer game, but I wanted to at least make an appearance."

"Oh Margaret, that's okay! I'm so glad you came. It means a lot."

"Please open it! I've been looking forward to giving it to you."

Lucy opens the bag and inside is a soft, floppy crocheted rabbit and matching cream baby blanket.

"Oh my goodness, did you make this?"

"I did."

"I didn't know you crocheted! They're both beautiful."

Margaret's eyes sparkle, and her wrinkles deepen as she smiles.

"I'm so glad you like it, and I hope this sweet little girl of yours loves it so much that it falls apart!"

Lucy reaches to hug Margaret. "Thank you so much."

"You're very welcome. Do you mind if I drop the meals off tomorrow afternoon?"

"That should be fine. We should be home. You really don't have to make us anything, though."

"I already made them. They're in my freezer waiting for you. See you tomorrow!"

As she watches Margaret walk away, Lucy takes a moment to look around the room. She can't stop smiling as her eyes fall on so many people she loves. For a second, she feels the usual combination of sadness, guilt and anger that her parents are not here too. She stops herself from going down that path again.

You know what- it's their loss. You are living your best life, and you have so many amazing people choosing to support you in it.

Lucy feels a weight lift off her chest, her mood noticeably improves, and her daughter kicks excitedly a few times. She grabs a cupcake off the table and walks back to join her village.

* * *

Later that night, as Lucy lays in bed she texts Bree.

"I know I said it earlier, but thank you for the baby sprinkle. It was perfect. Love you."

Bree texts back immediately in a series of individual texts.

"You're so welcome!"

"Love you too!"

"See you next weekend!"

Lucy smiles as she opens up the book on her phone, one hand resting peacefully on her stomach. Her daughter pushes against her hand happily. A few minutes later, Lucy is sound asleep.

Eloise

Eloise is just getting out of the shower when her phone rings.

"Hi, Mom. Can I call you back in a few minutes?"

"Eloise...Your dad."

Sobs overwhelm her mom's next words, and a rushing sound fills Eloise's ears.

"What's wrong? What happened?"

Eloise only catches bits and pieces, but it's enough.

"Leaving the bar... accident... gone..."

The rushing sound gets louder. She doesn't remember hanging up with her mom and the next thing she knows, she's standing in the living room wrapped in her towel as water droplets fall to the floor around her. Parker walks out of the kitchen with a mug in his hand. He stops when he sees her.

"What's wrong?"

"My dad. He died..."

"Oh, Eloise. I'm so sorry." Parker sets his mug down and wraps her in a hug.

She wasn't close with her dad. They had a complicated relationship and there were periods of her life she wished he wasn't even part of it.

But he was still my dad and the only one I'll ever have.

She buries her face in Parker's chest. The rushing sound quiets, replaced with weighted silence.

The next few days pass in a blur. Eloise feels like she's on autopilot as she helps her mom with arrangements. She's thankful for this though, because she isn't sure she could handle her mom's prickly mood otherwise.

They choose a casket.

"I don't know why it matters what it looks like when he's going to be cremated," her mom grumbles.

A flower arrangement must be picked for the top of the casket.

"Your dad would say he hated flowers, but you know he'd secretly want the most expensive ones."

They plan the meal for the funeral.

"Shouldn't someone be doing this for *us*?" her mom asks angrily.

"Oh, you mean it's inconsiderate to not help others in hard times- like asking a pregnant woman to help with her own baby shower?"

The only thing left is to write the obituary.

Of all the preparations, this one takes the longest. They sort through old pictures and mementos they hadn't known about but that he kept in a box in the closet. They found it while searching for clothes to give to the funeral home.

As they sift through his things, a piece of paper falls out. It's a drawing Eloise made for her dad for Father's Day when she was in elementary school. Two stick figures holding hands stare at them and childlike handwriting spells out, "Happy Father's Day!!!" Underneath this card are more drawings Eloise made throughout the years.

"I didn't know he kept these," she whispers.

"He must have thought they were good."

"He never told me that..."

"Well, you were a good artist."

Eloise catches the word "were" and realizes this is the only time her mom has complimented her art.

She looks at her mom and sees the dark circles under her eyes.

"Are you getting any sleep, Mom?"

"Of course I'm not," she snaps back. "How should we start this?"

They both stare at the blank notebook. What does one say about someone who had such complicated relationships? How do you write it in a way to not reveal that and to make it sound like you were closer than you actually were?

Tears burn her eyes, and Eloise closes them to stop them from falling. It was only within the last couple of years that she felt like she was finally building a positive relationship with her father.

I'll never know what could have been for us.

She takes in a quiet, shaky breath, too uncomfortable to cry in front of her mother.

As they sit in silence, Eloise wonders how many other obituaries are full of half-truths and regrets.

Lucy

Sleeping bags. Check.

Cooler. Check.

Flashlight. Check.

Drew's favorite stuffed animal. Check.

Lucy double checks her packing list to make sure they have everything they need for their vacation, a weekend camping trip with her sister's family. They started doing it a few years ago. They rotate who picks the location, plan meals together, and split the grocery bill. Honestly, most of the planning falls to hyper-organized Lucy, but she doesn't mind. It's always worth the work.

"Hey, Allen!"

"Yeah?" She hears him walk from the kitchen.

"Can you grab the medical supply kit from the top of the closet for me? I don't want to stand on a step stool right now in case I topple over."

"Like a weeble wobble." Allen smiles at her as he goes to the closet.

"Do people even know what those are anymore? I always say that too, but I don't think I've ever actually played with one. Did you?"

Allen doesn't respond and she looks over to see what he's doing. He's holding a weathered cardboard box labeled "Lucy." Water stains mark its corners.

"What is this?"

"My mom gave that to me after I went to college. She started cleaning my room so she could use it for extra storage."

Allen frowns, considering the timeline. "How long had you been gone?"

"I think it was during my first year."

Allen stares at her incredulously.

"Your mom cleaned out your room when you hadn't even been gone an entire year? Where did you sleep when you went home?"

"She kept my bed in the room."

"What did she do with the rest of your stuff? You had to have had more than one box?"

"She donated some of it. Probably threw some of it out."

"Your mom threw away things from your childhood... without talking to you about it first?"

"Tip of the iceberg, babe." Lucy chuckles uncomfortably as she continues folding items to put into the suitcases.

"How come I never knew about that?" Lucy glances toward him. Sympathy has flooded Allen's eyes and Lucy turns away so she can't see it.

"I don't know. I don't really enjoy thinking about it and it doesn't matter at this point. It was a long time ago."

"Did she at least tell you she was going through your stuff?"

"Kind of. When I came home for spring break, there was a pile of things on the floor of my room. She told me she'd been cleaning and that I should go through it to see what I wanted to keep."

"Wow..."

"Honestly, I didn't and don't really want any reminders of my childhood. I don't have a ton of happy memories. The only things I really wanted were my jewelry box and my Barbies so that I could give them to my hypothetical-future daughter, but she had already gotten rid of them when I came home."

Even though it's been fifteen years since that day the memory still stings, a perfect example of all the thought and care her parents showed while raising them.

Her childhood in a pile.

Checking her room top to bottom, twice, for some of her most prized childhood possessions.

Tears filling her eyes when she realized they weren't there.

She said nothing to her mom that day because she figured it was already too late, and she was so used to feeling unheard it wouldn't matter, anyway.

That spring break was a visceral reminder though of some of the dark moments of her childhood, and she can still remember it so clearly.

Her mom's first words as Lucy walked through the door, "You've thinned out so much!"

The day before she had to be back at school, when her dad told her they couldn't take her, and she needed to find a ride.

The old feelings of loneliness and depression came back, quickly and crushingly. It was the last time she would spend that long at her childhood home. She decided during that break, after leaving the heaviness of her home and parents for even that brief year of college, that she would probably have to keep her distance if she wanted to grow. At the time, she didn't think it would be this distant.

Tears come to Lucy's eyes now as she's transported back to the present. Allen is quick to notice. He sets the box down on the floor of the closet and wraps her in a bear hug.

"Oh, hun. I'm sorry."

"Bet you couldn't guess what you were getting into when you met me, huh? Our life was kind of f-ed up and I didn't even know it then."

"No shit. I'm so impressed with the person you are today."

"Thanks. I still have to remind myself that I am, too." Lucy smiles as she hugs Allen tighter.

Eloise

August

Eloise and Parker ride in the car on their way home from her father's funeral. The rushing sound returned during the service, and she couldn't even hear the pastor speak. It's finally quieted, and she now sits in the stillness.

Parker's eyes haven't left the road, and his hand hasn't left her knee. He occasionally rubs his thumb reassuringly across it. Her arms rest stiffly on top of her extended belly. She's so glad they're alone and away from all the pitying stares.

Her mother's eyes haven't been dry for the last two days. For someone who complained constantly about her husband and was so bitter during the funeral preparation, she certainly appeared distraught. Eloise wonders if her mother loves her father more than she realized, if she was acting to keep up the appearance of being a happy family, or if she just doesn't want to be alone.

I'll probably never know what she was really thinking.

It's then that Eloise realizes she hasn't cried yet today and doesn't feel like it.

She allows herself to sink further into the numbness.

The first place she goes when they get home is her daughter's future room. The air inside it feels stuffy, so she opens a window, and the singing of birds gets louder as she does. Bright sunlight filters through the tree branches, creating shadows on the wall.

Eloise stares at the blank space. Her eyes slide to a discarded notebook that sits on top of the desk. Next to it is her childhood jewelry box. Until now, she had the box in her own room but recently decided it should belong to her daughter.

She slips off her shoes and grabs the notebook. She sits in the rocking chair her mom gave her and starts doodling. As she draws, a design emerges. Eloise looks at the jewelry box again and then back at her paper. She holds the page up to the wall, imagining the design larger. She smiles slightly as she places the notebook back in her lap. Eloise feels tiny kicks press into her.

"You like this idea, huh? Me too."

Lucy

Lucy and her brother-in-law sit by the fire quietly, the two early risers in the family. The rest are still sleeping in the cabins, snuggled up in warm sleeping bags and fuzzy blankets.

Mist rises over the lake in front of their cabins and the sun is just breaking through the fog. The fire provides a comforting warmth against the chill of the morning air. It reminds her that summer is ending, but Lucy wants to hold on to these quiet, restful moments for as long as possible.

Erik flips the eggs in the large cast iron pan hanging over the fire. The blueberry muffins Lucy made are waiting in a container on the table. The kettle boiling in the coals whistles, and she carefully pulls it out. She pours the steaming water into the waiting steel French press and the smell of freshly brewed coffee rises from it.

"Is there anything better than hot coffee, a crisp morning, and this view?"

Before Erik can answer, one of the cabin doors opens and Allen comes outside, an enormous blanket snuggled close to his chest. He sits next to Lucy by the fire and Drew's sleepy eyes peek out at her.

"Good morning, buddy," she says as she gently brushes the hair from his forehead. She and Allen exchange smiles as their son's eyes close heavily.

Family members slowly emerge from the cabin, and they have a quiet breakfast as people wake up. They finish eating, clean up, and get ready to spend the first part of the morning hiking the trails of the campground. Lucy and Bree purposely picked this one because of its easy hikes, large playground and access to both a pool and lake.

"Lucy, do you want us to take Drew so you and Allen can rest? Or whatever you want to do." Bree winks at her.

"What else would they do?" Liam asks.

Bree whips around, not realizing her son was there. "Uh... Clean up the cabin."

"That doesn't sound as much fun." Liam's brow wrinkles and Lucy laughs as she finishes putting away the last of the breakfast.

"That would actually be great, if you don't mind."

"We don't mind! We'll take a walk and go to the playground for a bit. Hopefully, it warms up a little and they can go swimming this afternoon."

"We can take your kids to the pool to trade the favor, then."

"Super. Come on kids, let's go for a walk!" Bree yells as she wrangles the little ones.

Like herding cats.

As they walk away, Lucy feels a touch of panic. She calls out to Bree, "Keep a close eye on him, okay?"

"I know, Luce. I got it." She smiles and waves goodbye.

Once everyone has left, Lucy sits by the fire. The rhythmic sound of the waves quiets her mind.

Allen walks from the cabin, freshly showered. He moves a chair next to hers so their knees are touching. Lucy rests her head on his shoulder and they both stare out at the lake.

"How are you?" he softly asks.

"Fine. Tired."

"Do you want to take a nap?"

"Maybe. That sounds nice."

"Want me to join you?" Allen looks wolfishly down at her.

Lucy laughs and teases back, "Then I'm betting I won't get much napping done."

They settle into a comfortable silence, broken only by the sound of the waves and gulls.

"How are you feeling about the baby?"

"Good mostly, more nervous the closer it gets. I'm worried about Drew and how he'll react to getting less time with us."

"I think about that, too. We'll figure it out, though. We always do, and I'm sure most people feel that way when they have their second baby."

"I know. I bet he'll be the best brother to her."

Allen smiles into the top of Lucy's head. "I'm sure you're right."

"I also don't want to have a ginormous baby. Very worried about that, actually."

Allen snorts.

Lucy sighs and stands up. "I think I will take a nap."

"So am I joining you? You didn't answer me…"

Lucy laughs again as she walks toward the cabin. She stops halfway there and looks over her shoulder, smiling suggestively. "Come on, then."

Eloise

Eloise walks through the aisles of the craft store, deciding what material she wants to use for her artwork. She eyes all the colorful art supplies and feels her spirits lift.

She's never felt confident painting, so she skips those aisles entirely.

In high school, she loved drawing with charcoal, embracing the messiness of it and the shadows she could create. She decides she doesn't want something so dark for her daughter, though.

Crayons and markers seem too juvenile.

Eloise stops in front of the colored pencils. She's never used oil-based pencils before, but the idea of drawing richer, more vibrant pictures intrigues her. She grabs a seventy-two pack of pencils, a fancy eraser, and some oversize drawing paper.

Once she arrives home from the store, she clears off the dining room table and unwraps the supplies. Parker is at work and won't be back for hours. She turns on some music and recreates her sketch. She quickly becomes lost in her thoughts and the flowing lines she draws.

Eloise thinks about her dad. Memories (the good and the not so good) and what ifs play in her mind.

What if he had stopped drinking a long time ago?

What if I had tried to have a better relationship with him?

When was the last time either of us said "I love you...?"

She thinks about her mother too, now her only parent, and considers their relationship.

She won't be around forever either...

Her stomach twists at the thought.

How much time do I have to try fixing our relationship?

She thinks about her baby and imagines their life together.

What kind of mother do I want to be?

As if sensing her thoughts, she feels her daughter flip over. The movement makes her feel a little nauseous.

Okay, settle down, Baby Girl.

Despite all her parenting insecurities, she feels a deep connection to this little person inside her.

I will always be there for you.

She hears the key in the lock.

"Shit."

She wanted to clean up her work before Parker could see it, but she's lost track of time.

Too late now.

He sees her sitting at the table.

"What are you doing?"

"Drawing."

Parker comes closer so he can look at her work. She wrinkles her nose.

Is that...perfume...?

"What's it for?"

Eloise hesitates. "The baby's room."

Parker grunts before turning away.

She looks at the time and sees that his shift ended more than an hour ago.

"Where were you?" she asks curiously.

He answers without looking at her, "Stopped at the bar with a couple of the guys. I'm going to take a shower."

You have to be kidding me.

Lucy

"What's for dinner tonight?" Allen leans over Lucy's shoulder and rubs her back as he looks at the folding camp table in front of her.

"Pizza Tonka pies."

"Yes!"

"These first ones are ready so you can start cooking them."

Allen dances over to the fire, raising the cast-iron pans in the air. Lucy laughs at his excitement.

But I totally get it.

They're a family favorite and growing up she enjoyed hundreds of them around her grandparents' fire pit. Who would have thought that two pieces of sliced bread, pizza sauce, cheese and toppings baked in the coals of a roaring fire in the great outdoors would be such a delicacy?

That inventor deserves a MacArthur Genius Grant.

Even better are the apple and cherry pie versions they'll have for dessert tomorrow night. With a little cinnamon sugar sprinkled on top of the filling, they're the perfect treat. Lucy's mouth waters just thinking of them.

Bree comes out of the cabin and sees Allen still dancing. She chuckles. "Do you need help with anything, Lucy?"

"Yeah, can you get applesauce pouches for the kids? They're in the cooler."

Her nephew, Miles, runs past her with Drew chasing close behind.

"WALK when you're by the fire, you two!" she shouts at them.

"I'll watch them, hun."

"Thanks." She smiles at Allen as she continues to make the next set of pies. Bree comes back out of the cabin.

"Do you remember when Gramps tried adding double the filling that one time and the whole thing caught fire?"

Lucy laughs. "Of course. How could I forget? My hair smelled like smoke for days."

Both sisters are silent for a moment before Bree says, "I miss them."

"Me too."

"I think they'd be proud of us."

Lucy smiles back at Bree. "I know they would be. They were proud of us then, too."

* * *

"What's a pirate's favorite letter?"

"R!"

"Ahhh, you'd think it'd be the Rrrrr, but it's actually the C!"

Laughter echoes across the water.

Ingredients for s'mores litter the camping table. The wood in the fire pops and crackles. Long shadows appear on the grass as daylight fades into night. The first and brightest stars twinkle in the sky, which is deepening from light blue to deep plum.

Lucy sits next to Allen with his arm wrapped around her shoulders. She feels her daughter occasionally kick at her resting hands as her family members take turns telling jokes. Lucy looks at her son sitting next to her sister and nephews, his happy face sticky with marshmallow.

She leans her head onto Allen's shoulder and sighs in contentment.

She glances at her watch.

"One more joke, kids, and then it's time to get ready for bed."

"Awww! Can't we stay up late?" Liam complains.

Bree is quick to answer. "You're already staying up late!"

"Alright, I have a good one before bed. Are you guys ready?" Erik asks.

"Here we go," Bree says.

"What do scuba divers wear when they go to sleep?….. A snore-kel."

Lucy, Allen and Bree chuckle. Drew and Miles giggle loudly, not really getting the joke, but becoming wrapped up in the group's laughter, anyway.

Liam groans. "Dad, you're so lame."

Erik stands up and flourishes his arms in a dramatic bow.

Lucy and Bree stand up and start ushering their children into the cabins. After extra stories and snuggles to help them wind down from the day, all three are finally asleep. The adults return to the fire to talk quietly and, for everyone but Lucy, to enjoy an adult beverage.

A marshmallow stout would be perfect right now.

Eventually Allen falls asleep, his head nodding against his chest, and Erik takes that as his cue to go to bed himself.

"Don't stay up too late, you two."

He kisses Bree goodnight as Allen jerks himself awake with a loud snore.

"Guess I need to go to bed." Lucy and Bree laugh as he stumbles from his chair.

Lucy asks, "Do you need help getting there?"

They laugh harder as he shuffles clumsily to their cabin, and are then peacefully silent for a few minutes. The sounds of the crackling fire and tree frogs singing punctuate the still night. Lucy watches as embers rise gracefully up from the fire pit. One lands on an empty chair across from them before burning itself out quietly.

I wish it wasn't just us here...

"Do you ever think about getting back in touch with Mom and Dad?" Lucy says quietly into the darkness. She looks at Bree sitting beside her. Shadows from the flames dance across her face.

"I used to, all the time." Bree sighs. "But I also know that isn't what's best for me or my family right now."

Lucy pauses before adding, "They've been on my mind more with this baby coming." She looks down at her stomach and skims her hand across it as she replies, "What if they've changed? How would we know? I feel so guilty all the time."

"I know, and I do too. I have to remind myself that if they'd really changed, we would hear from *them*, though."

"That's true," Lucy says as she pulls the black plaid wool blanket tighter around her shoulders. She removes the band holding her ponytail in place. Her hair falls softly around her shoulders, covering her neck from the chill of the night air. "I miss having parents…but I don't miss our parents, if that makes sense."

"Yeah, I know exactly what you mean. If they haven't changed enough to reach out, do I really want them in my life? Why would I go looking for more negativity?" Bree asks with a slight edge of bitterness.

"And it's not like we haven't spent thousands of dollars and hours in therapy thanks to them."

"Exactly, and how much have they spent? I'm so sick of our healing being a one-way street." Bree moves her chair closer to the fire and tugs the hood of her sweatshirt up. "Right now my time and energy are so limited. I'm only investing in people who make me the best version of myself and who actually want to be part of my life."

"I get it. I feel the same way mostly."

Lucy stares quietly at the fire's comforting glow.

I just hope neither of us regrets that decision one day…

Eloise

Eloise sits at her dining room table with her art supplies in front of her. Her hand makes loose, sweeping strokes on the paper. She's lost track of the time again but has set an alarm to make sure she has plenty of time to clean up before Parker comes home.

Parker. That cheating SOB.

I don't have the bandwidth to even think about that right now with everything else going on.

She allows her thoughts to drift elsewhere and in what has now become usual for her, the creative process has given her a sense of calm and connection unlike anything she's ever experienced.

Why don't I always feel like this?

As she sits in the stillness, she remembers all the hours she used to spend alone in her room. She's always been more comfortable by herself.

Why is that?

Then it hits her.

Because her room was safe.

She was away from negative comments, away from bad moods, away from problems that weren't hers to solve (even though she always felt like she had to). As her hand makes another mark on the paper, Eloise remembers all the times she'd be home alone as a child. When she'd see her parents return, she'd immediately head to her room and close the door before they even came into the house.

Who was I avoiding, though?

Obviously, she was avoiding her dad's quick temper and any fights that would break out between her parents. She thinks about it further though and realizes she was also avoiding any criticism. Growing up, her father was such a powerful presence that she never realized how impacted she was by her mom, too. She always viewed her mom as the loving parent, the saving grace of the house. But now that her dad is gone and all that she has is her mom, now that she's finally given herself permission to explore her deepest feelings, she realizes that maybe her perceptions were clouded.

She thinks about her mom's moodiness and recent comments that have stung or made her feel self-conscious.

Was it always like that?

She tries to remember an earlier time. Was her mom different at some point? It's then that Eloise realizes she has few clear childhood memories of her mother.

Why is that? Did something happen that I blocked her out? Or were other memories just stronger?

She cannot answer these questions, and she's left with a feeling of unease.

Eloise turns her thoughts instead to her relationship with her mom now. She makes a long stroke with the pencil.

Our relationship isn't what I want.

But how do I change that?

Anxiety fills her stomach at the very idea of discussing her feelings with her mom.

Blackbird plays on her phone, and she quickly taps the alarm to turn it off.

Eloise finishes coloring in a petal before replacing the pencil in the box. She stares at her work so far and smiles, proud of what she is creating. Her daughter presses against her in a big stretch.

She grabs her phone and scrolls quickly through her social media, nearly passing by the People You May Know section. But she stops when her sister's smiling face catches her eye.

Eloise clicks on her name and starts swiping through the profile pictures. She notices how happy her sister looks in every single one.

Do I look that happy?

Impulsively she clicks on the Message button and sends her sister a quick note.

Hey! Saw your picture while scrolling. Your family is beautiful! I hope you're doing well!

She sets her phone aside and a small tear escapes her eye. She quickly wipes it away before it can fall on her art.

As she stands up, she hears her phone ding. She looks down at it and sees not only a reply, but a friend request from her sister. She quickly accepts and reads the reply.

Thank you! Miss you so much! Let's get together soon?

Eloise beams as she types back.

Lucy

Lucy approaches her university office door, returning for another school year. She balances a plant in one hand and her travel coffee mug in the other. She wedges her mug under her arm to unlock the door. As she sets the plant by the window, she checks the nest.

"Oh, no!"

It's empty.

She scans the tree, her breathing halted, and finally sees movement on the grass. A small black head pops out from under a bush.

"Oh!" she says, relieved that she didn't miss the baby birds totally.

The other two birds soon join their sibling. As she watches them stretching their wings, she thinks about how it won't be long before they're gone.

Her cheeks redden slightly with embarrassment.

They're just birds, Lucy... You don't have some deep emotional connection to them.

She opens her window quietly, so she doesn't startle the babies. It's hot, and the building is old without AC. Her room is stuffy, and she's just thinking how she should take her work outside to find a breeze when she gets a text from her sister. She assumes it's going to be a memory from their camping trip over the weekend.

Instead, she opens it to find an obituary.

Her dad's.

Time seems to stop for several seconds as her eyes rest on his name. She reads it again.

She scans the article quickly. It's short and details are sparse. She sees that the date is from a few weeks ago, and there was no funeral mentioned.

She texts her sister, "What happened?"

She sees her sister typing.

"I don't know."

More typing.

"I heard it was a drunk driving accident."

"But I also heard it was a heart attack."

Lucy sits for a minute in silence.

"I don't know what to say," she texts back.

"Me either ☹."

I knew this could happen, but didn't expect it to be so soon.

Tears sting her eyes, and her throat feels like she has swallowed a rough, hot coal. Before she has formed any thoughts, she's weeping, ugly crying in her quiet office. Deep, raw grief overwhelms her and her mind swirls with a flurry of emotions. One pushes its way aggressively to the surface, though, towering confidently over all the others. Lucy knows this emotion, too well, having wrestled with it for years.

Guilt.

Her breathing is shaky and her chest tightens uncomfortably. Tears continue to pour uncontrollably from her eyes.

I missed years with him. And I'll never get them back.

Lucy cries loudly as she remembers the few happy memories of him from her childhood…

Laughing as he told a joke.

Teaching her to swim.

Carrying her boxes to the car when she left for college.

She cries for her dad and the loneliness she imagines he experienced in his later years…

She pictures him sitting in the recliner, eating a TV dinner, staring at the television screen.

All by himself.

No one was there for him, including me.

Because he couldn't overcome his demons…

His yelling.

Her running.

Hiding.

She cries for herself and the father-daughter relationship she always wanted but never had…

She imagines talking with him about boy troubles.

Him telling her he loved her.

That he was proud of her.

Hugging him.

And now any chance of that relationship is gone.

Lucy cries for her kids and the grandpa that will never be part of their lives.

She can picture her dad with gray hair chasing Drew around the yard.

Him walking away, holding hands with her daughter.

I wish things had been different.

I could have tried harder.

I didn't have to set boundaries.

I could have reached out… Anytime.

Lucy takes a deep, ragged breath, trying to refocus.

You could have, but he could have too.

At this moment, though, regret restricts her breathing, as if she's suffocating. She breathes in deeply through her mouth and as she holds it, a quiet voice, an odd combination of Dr. Hadley's and her own, pushes its way through.

Setting boundaries is okay.

You can't control others' actions or choices.

And you don't have to like their choices or the result of them.

The reality that now the choice is final for her dad is unbearably heavy. Guilt returns to sit smugly atop the mountain of her emotions, the brief strength she felt momentarily crushed beneath it.

She cries until her shirt is damp and her eyes feel dry and gritty.

You made a hard decision to protect yourself and your family.

You were open to fixing things.

But you can't fix them alone.

Through hot eyes, she stares blankly out the window and sees one bird stand up. She watches as it beats its wings quickly a few times. It rises a couple of hesitant inches above the ground. She holds her breath as it topples forward and breathes out audibly as it rights itself. It stretch its wings once more and flaps them rapidly. Lucy watches the tiny bird fly away, initially clumsily, but then with more confidence and strength.

She smiles and closes her eyes. She takes several deep breaths through her mouth, dragging her confidence back to the top with each one.

Eloise

Rain pounds against the windows of the office building and droplets splatter across the cloudy, dirty glass. What began as a few showers throughout the day has now become a monsoon. Eloise is so engrossed in her work though she barely notices the storm outside.

In order to finish her picture before the baby comes, Eloise has had to work on it outside of the house and away from Parker. A few times a week, after her coworkers rush out the door at exactly five o'clock, she stays late and draws. She finds her daughter is most active when she's drawing and embraces all her kicks, punches and rolls.

The alarm goes off on her phone and as she moves to turn it off, she finally notices the heavy rain.

"Shit."

She's almost done with her picture and was hoping to take it home tonight to view it on the wall. She doesn't want it getting wet though, so she carefully rolls it back up and tucks it between her file cabinet and desk.

As Eloise packs up her things, she considers what her excuse for being late will be tonight. She always has believable reasons in case Parker is home when she comes back, which is honestly rare.

Her boss had paperwork she needed to finish.

She went to see her mom.

She had to run some errands after work.

Tonight she doesn't think it will be a problem because Parker mentioned going to the bar for dinner and beers with his buddies.

At least that's who he said it was with...

She continues to think of excuses as she gets into her car and then drives cautiously home. The road is slick and water pools dangerously across the pavement. She arrives at her house several minutes past the time she expected. As she steps onto her porch, water drips from her clothing. A chill runs across her skin while she fumbles with her keys.

Eloise unlocks her front door and walks into the dark living room. She turns the light on and jumps when she sees Parker sitting on the couch.

"What are you doing in the dark?"

"Waiting."

Eloise sees the empty beer cans littering the floor and table. She counts five in the few seconds she has to look. Parker walks toward her, and she can smell the beer on his breath before he even stops in front of her.

"Where were you?"

"I went out after work."

"Out? Out where?"

"To dinner."

"By yourself?"

Eloise can tell from his mood that she needs to be cautious with her answers.

"No, I was with Sarah."

Parker's eyes narrow.

"Where were you really?"

Eloise thinks quickly, trying to pull out the lies she came up with just a few minutes ago.

"Sarah and I went to the new pizza place on the other side of town."

Parker glares at her.

"Liar."

"Why would I lie about that?"

Parker takes a last drink of beer from the can and tosses it by the rest of the empty six-pack.

"You know, I'm starting to think you've been lying to me about a lot. Is the baby even mine, Eloise, or have you been screwing someone else behind my back?"

Even though this paranoia is new and alarming, she's furious at his ridiculous accusation and speaks before she fully thinks it through.

"Me? I'm not the one coming home smelling like someone else's perfume!"

Wrong move.

She sees Parker's eyes dilate and his jaw clench further. Before she can react, Parker's hands are on her. She feels his tight grip on her upper arm, squeezing deep into her muscle.

"Parker, stop! You're hurting me!"

"Shut up, bitch!"

Parker shoves her away roughly, causing her to lose her balance. Her shoes are still wet from the rain and squeak against the linoleum. She cannot catch herself and her body falls heavily to the floor.

Parker stands above her, shock slowly registering on his drunken face.

"Eloise... I'm so sorry. I didn't mean to."

Eloise stands up slowly and tries to assess if she's okay. Her arm stings and her tailbone is already aching from the fall. She doesn't feel the baby move.

Please move. Please be okay.

"Eloise, please look at me. I promise it wasn't on purpose."

Eloise stands still as Parker comes closer. He brings his face down near hers and she sees tears forming in his eyes. Tears mixed with fear.

But fear over what?

That he hurt me?

That he could have hurt the baby?

That he lost control?

"I'm so sorry, El. It won't happen again." Parker brings his arms up slowly to fold her into an embrace, and she lets him, hoping to keep his temper at bay.

But what if it DOES happen again?

Her daughter kicks once, hesitantly.

Thank God.

"I need to go to the bathroom," she says.

He steps aside, head hung low. As she walks down the hallway, she hears the couch squeak as he sits back down. She turns on the light in the bathroom and quietly closes the door. As she faces the mirror, she studies her face, trying to identify all the emotions on it- fear, shame, uncertainty.

"Ouch!"

Her daughter kicks her hard in the ribs, harder than she ever has before. She rubs the spot and looks down at her swollen belly. When she looks back at herself, she briefly spies an unfamiliar emotion.

Confidence.

She blinks back the tears racing down her cheeks.

I get it, Baby Girl.

Don't worry. I'll keep my promise to you.

Lucy

Lucy has taken a few days off from work to process her emotions.

She quietly leaves Drew's room after laying him down for a nap and then goes to the bedroom to turn the baby monitor on. She looks at her son on the screen, sleeping peacefully in his bed. As she turns away from the nightstand, she again sees the empty suitcases from their camping trip still sitting on the floor.

I asked Allen to put them away weeks ago. I'm so sick of looking at them.

Lucy sighs an unheard complaint and bitterly curses about it in her head. She opens the closet to see if there is space for them on the floor, knowing she can't lift them onto the shelf right now. She sees the "Lucy" box, forgotten where Allen had placed it before their vacation.

Lucy pulls the box out, rearranges a few things in the closet and then slides the suitcases inside.

She picks up the box and sets it on the bed, deciding what to do with it. It's been so long that she can't remember what's inside the box.

She opens it and finds her grandmother's obituary on top and underneath it is her grandpa's. She reads them both and smiles, flooded by the happy memories she shared with them. Their home was always a safe place for her.

She starts a to-keep pile by placing both pamphlets in a stack on the bed.

Returning to the box, she next finds a series of birthday cards from her parents. She doesn't remember keeping these and in her current life she's quick to recycle cards she receives after placing them on her mantle and acknowledging them for a respectable amount of time. Her mom kept every card she ever received in her closet, so Lucy grew up never throwing a card away either.

A ridiculous waste of space really.

She reads each of the cards and knows her mom's intent was always pure when writing them. She notices all of them are in her mom's writing and written from "Mom & Dad."

There are no items in the box from her father.

That doesn't mean he didn't love me. I'm just not sure how he showed it...

She starts another pile to throw away and places the stack of cards in it.

God, I hope there is no question in my kids' minds how much both *their parents love them. Ever.*

After removing all the cards, she gasps when she uncovers the next item, her old music box.

It wasn't lost after all.

Tears flood her eyes. She gently traces the hand painted lid and twists the knob carefully a few times before opening it. The familiar plinking tune fills the room.

Hot tears spill onto her cheeks as she realizes what song it plays, *Blackbird* by The Beatles. She never knew it as a child, and the box has been gone so long she had forgotten all about it.

The song finishes playing. She wipes her eyes and begins sifting through the music box's contents.

Inside, she finds a birthstone ring and other jewelry. She sets it aside for her daughter since they should share a birth month.

Unless this monster baby comes early...

Her daughter kicks her in the ribs, hard.

Just teasing, sweet girl.

Lucy finds a few rocks she collected as a child, ones deemed special enough to keep safe and hidden.

She reaches the light pink, velvet-lined bottom, lifting a stack of pictures from it. She holds the stack and starts looking at them one by one. Some she keeps, like the one of her and her sister playing dress up. They both wear princess pajamas and have cheap plastic tiaras on their heads and bright smiles on their faces. Others, especially ones where she sees the insecure, sad girl she used to be looking back at her, she throws away.

She closes the music box and places it carefully beside her on the bed. She returns her attention to the cardboard box to continue sorting items.

She sets her well-loved stuffed koala aside to be washed.

Maybe Drew would like it.

Her high school yearbooks are next and she reads the notes from her friends on the inside covers before also putting them in the to-keep pile.

She puts a faded T-shirt from a middle school field trip in the throwaway pile, on top of the greeting cards.

On the very bottom of the box are drawings from when she was in early elementary. The bottom most ones are water stained and some stick to the cardboard. She didn't tell Allen when he found the box that her mom had eventually taken it from her room to put in their basement. It had been on the floor and had gotten wet when the basement flooded one spring, obviously ruining some of its contents as well.

As Lucy looks through the papers she realizes she forgot how much she liked to draw as a little girl. Even though so much time has passed, she immediately remembers why she stopped, the memory sharp in her mind.

She was working on a school assignment and when she was finished, she asked her mom what she thought. Her mom took the picture from her tiny hands and laughed so hard she couldn't breathe. She didn't know why her mom was laughing and her mom never told her, but she knew it wasn't laughter that made you want to join in.

She never apologized for that.

I never told her how I felt though, either.

I hope my kids always feel comfortable talking to me, especially about their feelings.

Lucy looks at the drawings with fresh eyes now, ones that have seen a bigger world than her childhood home and recognizes the beginnings of talent in the drawings.

These aren't terrible.

Too bad I stopped drawing after that.

She sets the drawings aside, in the noticeably smaller to-keep pile.

She breaks down the box and takes it to the recycling. She pulls out a trash bag for the items she wants to throw away and then carefully picks up the music box. Lucy carries it into her daughter's room and sets it on the dresser, gently caressing its lid before leaving the room.

Eloise

Eloise arrives home from work to a quiet house, thankfully. She's been especially careful to not be late the last few days. They haven't spoken about the incident and the tension in the air has been thick. Parker has been overly affectionate and attentive, rubbing her swollen feet at night, having a cup of coffee ready in the morning and telling her he loves her before she leaves for work. She realizes that instead of finding it comforting she has found it stifling.

As she walks towards the kitchen, she sees flowers and a card on the dining room table.

El. Dinner tonight? - Parker

Eloise looks at the clock and sees that it's almost 5:30.

She sighs as she walks to her daughter's room to hide the drawing for now. Then she goes to her own bedroom where she searches through her closet for something a little nicer to change into. Her options are fewer as her bump gets bigger. She finds a flowy, casual dress she hopes will fit.

As she's putting it over her head, she hears Parker open the front door.

"Eloise?"

"In the bedroom."

She's standing in front of the mirror trying to decide if this dress is flattering enough when she sees his reflection walking down the hallway.

"You look great, hun."

"You don't think it makes me look chubby?"

Parker moves behind her and wraps his arms around her. He kisses her cheek and smiles at her in the mirror.

"I think you're the prettiest girl ever."

She's unfazed by this compliment from him that once would have made her blush.

"We should go. The baby is hungry."

Parker's arms fall from her shoulders. Eloise doesn't miss that at the word "baby," his expression hardened slightly before he fixed it.

Oh, that's right, my *baby is hungry. Much better.*

She grabs a sweater to put over the dress, both for the temperature and to hide the purple marks on her arm.

* * *

"This is nice." Eloise looks around the brightly lit restaurant and then across at Parker. She pulls her cardigan tighter around herself.

"I'm glad you like it."

Parker takes another long drink of his beer, his second already and their food hasn't even arrived yet. She thinks about how she's going to convince him to give her the keys so she can drive them home when their food arrives.

They make small talk as they eat, with Parker ordering another bottle every time he empties one. When the check comes, Parker pays, but she notices he leaves a rudely small tip. He gets up to go to the bathroom and Eloise tucks a few extra dollars in the book.

"Ready?" Parker asks when he returns to the table. His eyes are bloodshot and droopy.

"Sweetie, you look tired. It seems like you had a long day. How about I drive us?"

"Ssssure, swwwweets. That sounds good," Parker slurs as he slides the keys across the table. He smiles sloppily at her.

Thank God.

She smiles sweetly back, but it doesn't reach her eyes, not that he's in any state to notice.

Eloise drives them home and when they arrive, Parker goes into the bedroom. He lies down with his clothes still on and immediately falls into a drunken sleep. Eloise takes her time getting ready for bed, hoping Parker will be sleeping deeply by the time she's done.

When she finally gets into bed, Parker is snoring loudly beside her.

Eloise lies awake, shifting from side to side for hours, unable to quiet her thoughts.

The pottery studio flashes into her mind, and she envisions what it would be like to work there, seeing it so clearly it is like she can hear her footsteps echoing on the concrete and feel the clay in her hands. Next, a vision of her rocking her daughter appears. Eloise's drawing hangs on the wall. She can hear herself singing softly as she stares down at her baby and can see her daughter's bright eyes staring at her before her tiny lips break into the sweetest toothless smile. Eloise smiles back, her heart overflowing with love for the tiny human in her arms. She sees her mom leaning against the door frame, smiling as well. Eloise stands up and hands the baby to her. Before she does though, her mom embraces her warmly, careful to not hurt the baby in her arms.

The vision shifts, becoming more shimmery, and she can feel herself lying next to a man, not Parker, snuggled safely beside him.

The scene abruptly ends and Eloise stares at the blank wall in her bedroom. As her consciousness returns to reality, sadness and loneliness try to overwhelm her.

No. Not anymore.

Things have to change for me.

The baby kicks.

Oh yes, Baby Girl. For us.

Eloise pulls herself from the bed and leaves the bedroom, grabbing her phone on the way out. She quietly shuts the door, just as quietly opens the closet in the baby's room, and takes the paper into the kitchen. She carefully lays out the materials, selects a colored pencil, and starts working. Her plans and artwork flow effortlessly tonight as she finishes her drawing.

Lucy

Lucy sits in her university office, staring out the window. All three blackbirds have flown away. The view before her now feels boring and incomplete.

Again, just birds, lady.

Wild birds.

Not even pets.

She shifts her attention to her phone while she waits for her next class to begin. As Lucy scrolls through her social media page, an email notification pop onto her screen. She sees the sender and, unable to believe it, rereads it.

"Mom."

The subject line reads "Miss You…" She opens the email, curiosity getting the best of her, and starts reading.

"Hi,

I'm sure you've heard about your dad's passing. I've been thinking about you a lot and I would love to reconnect… I will leave the decision up to you… but I want you to know that I miss you… Hope to hear from you soon…

Love you,

Mom"

Lucy finishes reading and notes that there is no apology (*of course there isn't*), but at least there is no subtle guilt tripping.

She sits back in her chair, arms crossed, unsure of how to proceed. She is so sick of feeling guilty all the time for their lost relationship. Every day, she misses having a mom.

But do I miss MY mom?

Her phone lights up and she sees it's her sister.

"Did you get an email from mom too?"

"Yeah, just finished reading it."

"What are you going to do?"

Before she can reply, another message pops up.

"And why does she always use so many …? What the hell are they supposed to mean?"

Lucy chuckles and replies, "No idea."

What the hell am I supposed to do with this?

Lucy rereads the email, the first of many times she will do so.

Gonna get my money's worth in therapy this week.

"…"

As Lucy's thoughts circle around her mother's email, she pictures herself sitting with her mom. She looks the same as she did the last time she saw her, but seems more tired and… sadder? Lucy can't tell for sure. She watches her mom lean far back in her chair, as emotionally unavailable as she remembers her being.

Lucy blinks and sees the email again.

Has she changed?

Is she willing to listen to me now?

Eloise

Eloise stands in her living room and scans for cleanliness.

Carpet vacuumed.

Bathroom cleaned.

Kitchen clutter stashed away.

Throw pillows fluffed.

To her eyes it looks pristine.

I hope Mom doesn't start cleaning before I even begin this conversation.

Eloise walks into the kitchen to cook. She awkwardly bends down to get a pot, her thighs hitting against her belly. Just as dinner is finishing, she hears her mom knock on her door. She wipes her hands on the kitchen towel and goes to open it for her.

"Hi, Mom."

"Hey, hun! I brought some salad." Her mom bustles past her.

"Thanks, but you didn't have to do that. Dinner is almost ready."

"Good, I'm hungry. I haven't eaten all day."

"Why not?"

"Oh, I started a new fasting diet."

Eloise turns back into the kitchen, shaking her head.

"Speaking of diets. I saw Tiffany Baker. She's gained so much weight! She used to be so small." Her mom's eyes are wide with horror.

The absolute worst tragedy to occur to someone in her mother's eyes is a person increasing their pant size.

"Huh. This is done."

They get their plates and sit down at the table. Eloise notices that her mom's plate is ninety percent of the salad she brought. There's only a small corner of the plate with the food Eloise prepared.

They make semi-uncomfortable small talk before settling into a minute of silence. Eloise knows she needs to speak before her mom tries to fill it.

"Dad passing made me think about a lot of stuff."

Her mom glances up from her own plate. She doesn't reply, so Eloise pushes forward.

"I've realized I was really hurt by things that happened in my childhood." Eloise takes a deep breath. "And I'd like to have a better relationship with you from now on."

"What do you mean 'better'? What's wrong with our relationship?" her mom asks critically. Eloise can already sense the tension rising in the room.

"I just mean there's a lot I never said growing up and even as an adult. I don't think it's healthy for me to bottle everything up." Another deep breath. "And I hope you'll be willing to listen to how I'm feeling."

"You don't think I listen to you?"

The wheels are starting to come off...

You can still save it though if you're careful.

"I don't mean that. I just mean that I've never felt comfortable being totally honest about my thoughts and feelings, not just with you, with everyone, and I'd like for that to change."

"Why don't you feel like you can be honest with me?" The accusatory tone is less than welcoming.

"Well." *Don't chicken out now.* "I don't think our home was one where people were free to speak their minds. I walked on eggshells a lot and it was just easier to keep everything to myself."

Her mom puts a piece of bright green lettuce into her mouth and chews slowly. Eloise looks down at her plate, waiting, unsure if she should add more.

"Well, I'm sorry you had such a bad childhood."

I knew she'd say something like that.

I just want to have an honest, adult conversation for once.

"I didn't say that," Eloise says, biting back irritation.

225

"You may as well have. You sound exactly like your sister." Her mom shakes her head angrily. "You know other kids grow up in much worse homes. We maybe didn't have a ton of money, but you were always taken care of."

Before she can reply, her mom stands up and takes her plate to the sink.

"I should go. I have laundry to do at home."

Eloise watches silently as her mom collects her purse and puts on her shoes. "Thanks for dinner. I'll talk to you later."

"Bye," Eloise says shortly as the door closes loudly. She finishes her meal alone, replaying the conversation in her mind over and over. Her anger cools some each time, gradually being replaced with the first traces of regret.

Did I just lose my mom for good, too?

Lucy

Lucy arrives home from her clinic early after the last patient for the day canceled their appointment.

I need to update my cancellation policy.

She decides to use the precious alone time to finish the chores that have been hanging on her to-do list all week.

As she waters her plants on the porch, she sees Drew's tortoise planter and notices the succulent is overflowing from its container. She decides if it needs to be replanted, she may as well take the succulent inside before the weather turns colder.

When all of her plants have had a long drink, she takes the tortoise inside the garage. She sets it on the dusty workbench and dreams of the day she has a beautiful she-shed to garden and read in.

That's when I'll know I've really made it, baby.

Lucy feels the comforting quiet and peace that always settles over her when she's alone and taking care of her plants.

She allows her mind to wander, and it drifts to the email from her mom. She showed it to Allen, but Drew interrupted them and they haven't returned to the conversation.

I didn't feel happy to hear from her. Not really, anyway.

She pours a little dirt into the bottom of a new pot.

I felt angry and bitter.

She moves the tortoise in front of her and shakes the dirt loose so she can release the plant from its now too small container. Like Drew, the plant seems to have grown a ridiculous amount this summer.

She could have reached out for years and didn't.

Why now?

Does she need something from me?

The plant is reluctant to leave its comfortable home. She picks up a spoon and more aggressively than she intended, uses it to release the roots. A small piece breaks off.

Easy, killer.

Lucy softens her prying, and the plant finally gives up its fight and lifts from the pot.

You've been waiting years to hear from her. Do you really want to be the one to slam the door on that relationship?

While she has it out of the pot, she sees that some leaves on the bottom have died. She removes them to better help the new growth.

What would starting a relationship with her look like right now?

When she's removed the last of the dry, crinkled leaves, Lucy centers the plant in the new pot and scoops handfuls of dirt around it, settling it safely into its new home. She brushes off the dirt from the top of the planter. She's always amazed at how much bigger plants look when they're taken out of their cramped pots.

What do I want that relationship to look like?

Lucy pictures talking easily with her mom.

Laughing with her.

Crying with her.

Her mom snuggling Drew.

Rocking her daughter.

She sets the plant aside and starts cleaning up her work area.

Is that relationship really possible, though?

She shakes the dirt off her planting mat, folds it up and returns it, the potting mix, and her other tools to the shelf.

I don't want to feel hurt by her again.

As she reaches for the newly potted plant, the familiar glimmers appear. She sees another hand and arm. Unlike her tanned arms, thanks to all the hours she's spent outside with Drew this summer, this arm is pale in comparison. As the arm moves forward, she can see up to the bicep and dotting it are a few faint purple splotches. Lucy blinks and sees the planter in front of her again. She holds onto the table and takes a moment to ground herself.

These really don't seem like hallucinations...

She feels her daughter shift around the knot of anxiety in her stomach.

What if one happens when I'm driving, though?

I should talk to Dr. Hadley again.

She then carefully picks up the plant and goes into the house where she places it on an end table in the living room. She glances at the clock and sees that it's almost time for her to leave to get Drew.

* * *

"Hey! Where this plant come from?"

Lucy stops unloading the dishwasher and peeks out into the living room and to find Drew pointing at his succulent.

"That's your succulent, hun." She turns around.

"Mom!"

She hears her son's distraught wailing from the living room. "Oh, boy."

"What's wrong, Drew?" She leaves the kitchen and sees her son standing by the end table, anger and disappointment clouding around him.

"What happened to my turtle plant?"

"I had to put it in a bigger pot."

"Why?!?"

"Because your plant got bigger and needed a bigger pot."

Her son continues to glare at her angrily.

"Okay..." *How would Mr. Rogers explain this...?*

"It's like when you get bigger. When you grow, you need bigger pants. The pot is like the plant's pants."

Her son's glare softens before turning into a mischievous smile.

"The dirt is its underwear, right?" He starts laughing and Lucy automatically joins in.

"I think you're right."

She hears chuckling behind her and turns to see Allen standing in the doorway. They exchange smiles.

"Dada!" Drew races over to him and Allen scoops him into his arms.

"Hey, buddy. How are you?"

"Good! Did you know dirt is plant pants!?!?"

"I heard that!" His eyes twinkle as he carries Drew over to Lucy. He greets her with a kiss.

"Hey Dada, can we go outside to pay?"

"Sure, buddy. Let's find your shoes."

As they pass by her, Lucy mutters, "Close one. Barely avoided another world war there."

Eloise

Eloise is home alone for the weekend. Parker is taking one final summer camping trip with his brother (*allegedly*) to stake out some hunting grounds for the fall. She didn't think it was worth mentioning that they'd have a newborn during hunting season this year.

Because 1. He won't care and 2. Hopefully, we won't be around him much longer. As soon as I figure out the details.

Today, Eloise invited Sarah shopping with her so she could buy a few more things for the baby's room.

And hopefully she has some ideas to help me get out of this mess.

They've already been down the baby aisle and all she has left to purchase is a frame for her picture.

"What about this one?" Sarah holds up a thick black frame.

"No. I think I want something lighter."

"Like that?" Sarah points to a rustic light brown one.

"Less like I found it in a barn."

Sarah holds up a thin gold frame, an antique floral pattern lines the outer border.

Eloise smiles.

"Perfect."

As they turn the corner of the aisle, Eloise nearly bumps into a man. He sees her first and puts his arms out to stop them from colliding.

"Hey! It's you again!" she hears him say as he pulls her away lightly.

Eloise looks at his face, her eyes locking with his bright blue ones. Several long seconds pass before she recognizes him.

231

Brian from the hardware store.

"You should take better care of yourself and watch where you're going!"

Eloise chuckles and gestures to her stomach. "I must have forgotten my caution tape belt today."

Brian laughs and continues walking.

Sarah clears her throat to get Eloise's attention and raises her eyebrows meaningfully.

She whispers, "Who was that? He's cute!"

"Yeah, I'm not really in any position to notice that."

"Sure you are. I don't see a ring on your finger, or on his actually. He seems nice."

Sarah winks at her as she pushes their cart to the checkout. Eloise follows behind her but first looks toward the aisle where Brian disappeared.

He does *seem nice...*

When they get home, Sarah helps unload the car. Eloise's stomach is in the way of most things these days, and it feels comforting to have someone help her.

"I'm going to put this in the baby's room," Eloise says as she carries the frame and the rolled up drawing down the hall.

"Okay, I need to go to my car to get something. I'll be right back."

Eloise unrolls the paper and gently places it in the frame. She struggles to hold it down as it tries to re-curl itself.

Hopefully, the frame is tight enough to flatten it.

She finishes placing her drawing carefully inside and turns it over to look at it. It's perfectly flat and honestly stunning. She's so proud of her work that she can't help smiling.

Sarah comes into the room carrying a gift bag and sees Eloise standing in front of the drawing.

"Oh, El. It's beautiful." She looks from the drawing to Eloise's smiling face. "I'm so proud of you. Your daughter is going to love it."

"Thanks. I love it too."

"I have something for you."

"You do?"

Sarah hands her the bag. Eloise pushes the tissue paper aside to uncover a soft crocheted blanket tucked around a matching crocheted teddy bear.

"Oh, my goodness," Eloise says quietly.

"My grandma makes them."

"Wow. It's lovely. Thank you, Sarah."

Eloise places them on the dresser beside the jewelry box for now.

"Do you want some help hanging your picture on the wall?" Sarah asks her.

"That would be great. Thanks."

Eloise leaves the room to find a tape measure, nail and hammer.

When she comes back, Sarah is cleaning up the tissue paper and bag. Eloise breathes deeply and asks, "Hey, can I talk to you about something? About Parker?" She clears her throat. "I need ideas... and maybe some help."

Sarah looks up quickly, hearing Eloise's nervous but certain tone. With a reassuring look she replies, "Absolutely. What do you need?"

Lucy

September

The cafe is quiet, which normally Lucy would like. She could use some more background noise to help drown out her buzzing thoughts today, though. She sits in front of the window and lets those walking by distract her.

Lucy rereads what she's typed. Again. She's finally drafting a reply to her mom's email, but is still not sure exactly what she wants to say. She has typed and retyped each sentence at least four times each.

I'll meet with her.

But not until after the baby comes next month.

I don't want her knowing I'm pregnant or meeting Drew yet.

Her fingers hover over the keyboard.

Should I suggest we start with a phone call?

I could do that now...

She stares out the window without really seeing.

Am I ready for it now? *Or do I need to sit with this longer?*

She finally notices a black shape flying back and forth in front of the window. She focuses on it and realizes it's a small blackbird.

Is that one of my baby blackbirds? Would it have flown all the way here?

As she gazes at it, her sight becomes blurry. Instead of shimmery though, the image is hazy and unfocused. She can make out rough shapes, but it's not as clear as these experiences normally are.

She feels herself standing beside a blurry Drew. He's taller and older, a teen or young adult. She reaches her arms toward him and hugs him tightly,

234

pressing him against her body.

He pulls back and starts walking away, toward a misty group of people. They're all interacting happily- laughing, smiling, hugging, arms around one another. A bright light rises above them, and Lucy feels its warmth. It's strangely familiar and reaches deep within her, like the chords of a favorite song humming through her bones.

Just before Drew reaches the crowd, he turns back, grins, and gestures for her to follow.

She hurries toward him, closing the gap quickly.

He places his arm around her shoulder and squeezes her lovingly.

A young woman walks toward them and places her hand in Lucy's. She's never seen her before, but Lucy knows she's her daughter. As Lucy stands between her children, she feels different. Her breath catches when she realizes she doesn't feel like their protector, but instead is their companion.

"Evie!"

Lucy is pulled from the vision by the barista calling out an order. Her daughter kicks her sharply.

She blinks and looks around. The blackbird is gone from the window. She breathes out and her chest feels lighter than it ever has before.

She deletes the email she's written and starts again.

Eloise

Eloise is vacuuming when her phone lights up with a call. She considers ignoring it until she's done, but when she sees it's her mom calling, she turns off the vacuum and runs as fast as she can to answer it.

"Hello?" she asks tentatively and breathlessly.

"Hi."

Silence on the other end.

"How are you?" Eloise asks to get the conversation started.

She hears her mom sigh deeply.

"I thought about what you said."

Eloise holds her breath. She didn't expect her mom to self-reflect, let alone so quickly.

"I'd like to work on our relationship, too."

Eloise breathes out in relief.

"Oh!" she says before she can check herself. "Good. That means a lot."

"I know I don't say it often, but you're important to me. You're my daughter, and you should be able to be honest with me about everything. I'm sorry you haven't felt that way your whole life." Her mother's voice breaks slightly with emotion. Eloise's eyes tear up. "I decided that it's important I tell you that before you become a mother yourself soon."

"Thank you," Eloise replies. It's all she can say as emotion and surprise overwhelm her. It's more than she ever expected to hear and more than she's ever heard her mother say before.

"I already lost one daughter, and I don't want to lose another."

"Maybe it isn't too late... if you try reaching out to her."

Eloise doesn't reveal that even though they haven't found time to meet, she's been talking with her sister again.

She doesn't seem angry. I think she may be willing to reconnect.

Loud knocks sound at the door, covering up her mom's reply.

"Mom, I have to go. Someone's about to bang my door down. I'll call you back later, okay?"

"Okay, I love you."

Tears flow freely down her face as Eloise replies, her voice breaking, "I love you too."

KNOCK KNOCK KNOCK.

She opens the door quickly and standing outside is a police officer. Close-cropped graying hair peeks out from under his hat and his tall figure casts a long shadow in the doorway. Despite his mildly intimidating appearance, he has a grandfatherly presence.

"Hello, ma'am. Does Parker Southwood live here?"

"Yes."

Did something happen to Parker?

"Is he here now?" the officer asks.

"No, he's out."

"Do you know where I can find him?"

If he isn't dead, did he do something stupid? Is he in trouble and that's why the cops are here looking for him?

"No, he's gone camping, and I haven't heard from him."

"Can you please tell him that Officer Bradford was here and that he needs to get back with me right away?"

"Sure, can I ask what this is about?"

"He missed his parole meeting with me this week."

Parole meeting?

She knew Parker had trouble with the law before, but she didn't know he was on parole.

The officer looks behind her and sees the empty beer cans on the counter. He glances at her undeniably pregnant belly.

He softens his tone and asks, "I'm going to bet those aren't your cans?"

Eloise looks behind her and pauses before answering. She can't lie to a police officer. She doesn't want to get Parker in even more trouble, though.

Not that I should care at this point.

Before she can respond, Officer Bradford interrupts her thoughts.

"Ma'am, it isn't my place, but if I were you, I would consider my best options right now."

The officer stares at her intensely but kindly. "Please let us know if we can help with...anything. Have a good day."

"Thank you, Officer."

She closes the door softly and leans against it for only a second. She leaves the rest of the cleaning undone and walks quickly to her bedroom to lie down for a while and to think.

Eloise sits on the bed and feels her baby's tiny kicks pressing into her. She lightly rubs her stomach, feeling the kicks move closer to where her hand is resting. She pulls out her phone and checks her bank account.

Will that be enough? It might be if I don't have to pay for daycare...

Eloise lays down and closes her eyes, falling asleep to the gentle rhythm of her child's movements.

While she naps, she dreams. Eloise stands underneath a large tree at the same park she saw in her dream from months ago. The blackbird flies freely overhead. She gazes up at it and then hears a little voice calling her soon-to-be-name.

"Mom!"

She turns and smiles.

Lucy

Lucy picks Drew up from daycare to take him shopping with her after work. In the store parking lot, she wrestles him out of his car seat, made more challenging by her stomach that is now constantly in the way. She sets him on the ground and grabs his hand.

"Okay, buddy. Let's get a new plant for Sister's room and then we'll go find a snack."

Lucy and Drew walk into the home goods store.

"Mama! Look!" She follows his point to see a display of stuffed animals.

"Oh, look at those. Do you want to pick one out for you and one for Sister? You can give it to her as a welcome home gift."

"Yeah!"

As Lucy and Drew search through the shelves, she hears her name.

She turns around to see Margaret walking toward her. She waves at Drew and Lucy stretches out her arms to hug her, awkwardly of course with her stomach creating a gap of several inches.

As Margaret pulls away from her, Lucy notices she is wearing a charm bracelet with a blackbird attached.

"Margaret, I've never noticed that charm before."

Margaret looks down at her wrist.

"I rarely wear jewelry when I'm gardening, so you've probably never seen it."

"That's so funny. Blackbirds keep coming up in my life at the most random times," Lucy says.

"My husband gave it to me. We used to love birdwatching together, and blackbirds were one of Winston's favorites." Margaret touches the charm gently and rubs it delicately between her fingers. "They're actually pretty neat birds. Did you know blackbirds have–"

"Mama! I want the giraffe!"

Margaret smiles at Drew as he holds up a plush giraffe. "I'll stop rambling on about birds and let you two finish your shopping. Bye, Drew!" She smiles and waves goodbye to him before walking away.

Lucy returns her focus to him. "Which one are you picking for Sister?"

"Hmmm." Drew looks through the animals again and grabs a white tiger. "This one!"

"Great choice, bud. Let's go find a plant now."

"What?!? Another one?!?"

Lucy chuckles.

"You're as bad as your father."

* * *

Lucy walks in the door holding Drew's hand and carrying the plant they picked out.

"What the heck is that?!?" Allen asks her.

She laughs. "Calm down. It's for the baby's room."

Lucy sets the tall, pointy plant on the kitchen counter.

"Every room needs a snake plant," she says.

Allen wrinkles his brow skeptically. "Really? Why's that?"

"I read some NASA study that said they help with air purification. I don't know how true it is for an entire home, but they look nice and are super low maintenance, which is perfect for this crazy season of life we're in."

"Great." Allen gives her a sarcastic thumbs up.

Lucy laughs. "Can you get the other bags from the car? My feet are hurting, and I'd like to take my shoes off. I think my feet have gotten bigger again. I'm about to need clown shoes."

"If there's another plant in your car I'm leaving it outside."

"Guess you'll just have to go see huh?" Lucy winks at him. She feels a small cramp in her pelvis, the second one today. She turns away before Allen can see the worry that has suddenly appeared on her face.

Eloise

She wakes up from her nap to a door slamming.

"Eloise!" Parker yells.

Uh oh.

She slowly gets out of bed and places her hand under her stomach to support herself. She shuffles from the bedroom, meeting Parker in the hallway.

He gestures to the sink, still full of dishes.

"Why isn't this room clean?"

She can smell the cheap beer on his breath as he comes closer.

Be smart here. Don't make the same mistake as last time.

She stays silent and looks at the wall past him.

"Answer me."

He pushes her just enough to make her lose her balance. She takes a step back to steady herself. Her baby stretches, reminding her it is no longer just her she must think about.

Never again.

"Don't touch me," she says quietly, head down.

"What did you just say?" Parker steps in front of her face. Her heart beats faster. Her daughter kicks twice.

Kick.

Kick.

Don't worry, Baby Girl.

She slowly looks up and makes direct eye contact with him.

You can do this.

"I said, don't touch me."

Parker takes a step back but raises his arm slightly.

"Touch me and I'll call the cops."

Something in her tone makes him stop. He turns his head to the side slightly.

He chuckles disbelievingly. Parker smiles drunkenly and starts walking towards her again. She can't tell if he's going to push her or kiss her, but she doesn't care either way. She takes a step back.

"Get out," she says. Her voice shakes, but there's a confidence to it she's never heard before.

"What?"

"Get. Out. I don't want you here. We don't need you."

"Aww, sssweeets. Don't be like that."

"Give me your key and get out or I'll call the police. I know you don't want them coming here and seeing you like this. Your parole officer would find out, and then what?"

Parker stops moving and stares at her.

"Are you seriousss? Where am I ssssupposed to go?"

"I don't know, and I honestly don't care. Text me before you come back for your things so I can have someone here with me."

"Fuck you," he says as he throws his key ring at her.

He stumbles toward the door. "Don't call me when you need help."

Eloise laughs sarcastically.

"What the hell would I need your help with?"

The door slams behind him and Eloise rushes to lock it.

She sits on the couch and breathes a sigh of relief.

Then she bursts into tears, ones she's been holding back for months.

After several minutes, she takes a deep breath. She goes into the bathroom and splashes cold water on her face and blows her nose. She looks at her puffy eyes in the mirror and the thought that has been in the back of her mind for weeks springs forward again.

She returns to the living room, picks up her phone, and dials a number.

"Hello, CB Pottery. How can I help you today?"

"Hello, my name is Eloise Murray, and I interviewed for a job a few months ago. I'm wondering if it's still available."

Kick-kick-kick-kick.
She smiles in response.
We've got this, my sweet girl.

Lucy

Lucy nervously sits in her OB's exam room for one of her last routine appointments. She's been experiencing more cramping the last two days, and she's concerned it's signs of early labor. She knows it's too soon, so she hopes Dr. Burman can give her some answers and ease her worries.

Her doctor enters and smiles at her warmly. "Hi, Lucy. How are you today?"

"I've been better."

Dr. Burman focuses on Lucy's tight face, waiting for her to say more.

"I think I've been having contractions."

"That's pretty normal to have some false labor. How often are they happening?"

"At least once a day. Sometimes a few times in a row over an hour. They're never consistent, though."

"Okay. I rarely do a physical exam at this stage of pregnancy, but given your last pregnancy and labor, I think I'd like to check you today, as long as you're alright with that."

"That's fine." Lucy feels equal parts relief and added anxiety.

Dr. Burman continues to ask her questions, takes measurements, and finally, they listen to the baby's heartbeat.

"Sounds great, Lucy. Baby is still measuring a couple of weeks ahead."

Of course she is...

Lucy wipes the sweat from her palms onto her maternity jeans.

Dr. Burman stands up to leave the room. "I'm going to have you undress just your bottom half and we'll do a quick check. I'll give you a couple of minutes to change."

Once the door closes, Lucy undresses and returns to the exam table.

Please let everything be fine. Let it just be false labor.

She carefully covers her lower half with the papery sheet left out for her. Her thighs are slick with nervous sweat, and she hurriedly tries to wipe it on the crinkly exam paper.

Like Winnie the Pooh here. Top and no pants.

Another knock sounds on the door. It opens slightly and Dr. Burman calls inside, "All set?"

"Yup."

She enters the room and starts putting on a glove.

"Okay, let's see what's going on."

Lucy shifts slightly as she adjusts to the doctor's gentle but still uncomfortable poking and prodding.

"Ohhhhhkay. Well, you're dilated to a three…. almost three and a half so those contractions are doing something."

Lucy's breathing quickens.

Dr. Burman removes her glove and tells Lucy she can sit up. The doctor returns to her stool and writes a note on Lucy's chart. When she looks up, Lucy notices her eyes are slightly wider than before. Her next words come a little quicker and with more urgency.

"How often did you say the contractions are happening? Daily?"

"Yes, sometimes just once a day, but other times more."

"I want you to monitor them closely, okay? When they happen, I want you to drink a glass of water to make sure you're well-hydrated."

"Okay."

"IF they become more frequent or you notice any bleeding or fluid loss, call us right away. If they're ever consistent enough to be five minutes apart and it lasts for at least thirty minutes or if your water breaks, I want you to call the hospital and tell them you're coming so I can meet you there."

Lucy's breathing has become more spastic.

It's too soon for her.

She needs more time.

"How long do you think I have? This feels way too early," she asks, anxiety clear in her voice.

"It is early. If we can get you to thirty-six weeks, I'll feel better."

Better.... That's a loaded word here.

Dr. Burman continues, "The good thing is the hospital has a NICU, so you can be with her as soon as you're cleared to without having to be discharged. Do you have other questions?"

"No, I don't think so."

"Okay, we'll hook you up to the monitor for a bit before you leave just to be safe. Unless something is concerning, the nurse will read it for you, though. Take it easy, Lucy, and please let us know if anything changes, okay? I'll see you next week for your next appointment." Dr. Burman smiles at her warmly, but smaller than typical, before leaving the room.

I hope I don't see her before that.

I need to make it at least one more week.

Eloise

Eloise knocks on her boss's door first thing in the morning.

"Mr. Frank, can I talk to you for a minute?"

Her boss looks up from his phone, and Eloise sees Candy Crush on the screen.

Obviously I'm interrupting something SUPER important here.

"Sure, Eloise. What can I help you with?"

Eloise takes a seat in front of his desk.

"You obviously know I'm pregnant." Eloise smiles, but Mr. Frank looks at her questioningly, wondering what is coming next. "I want to say how appreciative I am of my time here. I decided that after the baby is born though, I want to try a different job."

"You do?"

"Yes. I've always loved art, and the pottery studio is hiring. They offered me the job, and it seems like a good opportunity, especially because it would help me with childcare."

"Wow. Well, I can't say I blame you then. I'm sad to see you leave though, Eloise. You've been an exceptional employee all these years."

"Thank you."

"If you ever change your mind, we'd love to have you back."

Eloise thinks about the quiet, nearly empty office and wonders how much longer they will even be open.

"Thank you, I appreciate that."

"Best wishes, Eloise. Let me know if there's anything you need from me." Her boss stands up and extends his hand to her.

She accepts his handshake and thanks him. Before she's even left his office, she sees him grab his phone, the game still blinking on it colorfully. She shakes her head on the way out the door.

Eloise sees Sarah's desk is empty and searches the small office for her. A few seconds later she finds her in the breakroom pouring herself a coffee.

"I have some news."

"You're pregnant?"

Eloise laughs lightly.

"Besides that." Eloise sits down at the table. "I just got done talking to our boss."

Eloise pauses dramatically, and Sarah waits for her to continue.

"I told him I won't be coming back after the baby is born."

"You aren't? What are you going to do instead?"

"There's a job opening at the pottery studio. I interviewed for it, and they offered it to me."

"Wow, El! That's great!" Sarah hugs her and beams at her. "I didn't know you did pottery."

"I don't, but they're willing to teach me." She tells Sarah a little about the job, excitement coloring her voice.

"This sounds perfect. I'm so happy for you!"

"And one more thing- I kicked Parker out over the weekend."

Sarah's eyes widen with mixed surprise and concern.

"Did something happen? It's sooner than I thought you'd decided to do it."

"I couldn't take it anymore. This baby is the most important thing to me and I'm not letting her grow up worse or even the same as I did. I'm choosing to do better for her."

"Eloise, this is all amazing. I'm so proud of you!"

"Thanks. Me too."

"We'll need to have celebratory drinks after the baby comes!"

Eloise laughs. "I don't need a drink to celebrate, but if you'd like to get me a gift, you can watch the baby for a couple hours while I sleep."

"Deal. Hey, I wanted to ask, I'm going to a Sips and Succulents class this Saturday afternoon. Do you want to come? It's BYOB, so you can bring whatever beverage you want."

Eloise feels a flicker of interest and without hesitation she responds, "Yes! I don't have any plants, but that sounds fun."

"Great! I'll double check the time and we can figure out when we want to meet."

"Perfect. Maybe we can get coffee before or dinner after."

"I'd love that. Maybe even both!" Sarah's desk phone rings in the other room. "I'll get back to you with details before I leave today."

On her way out of the breakroom, Eloise sees an empty cardboard box waiting to be recycled. She grabs it before heading to her own desk. She tucks it underneath to use for packing later.

Lucy

Lucy steps out of the shower. Her stomach tightens again.

I don't think I'm going to make it to my next appointment...

She looks at the clock on the wall.

At least I made it to thirty-six weeks.

Barely.

But what if that's not enough?

After she has finished drying off and getting dressed, she blow-dries her hair. As she is wrapping up the cord and placing the dryer back in the drawer, she grips the edge of the sink as another contraction comes.

Nine minutes.

"Allen!"

Is she fully developed?

What if her lungs aren't ready?

She hears his footsteps walking quickly to her and sees him peek into the bathroom, his eyes tense.

"We need to get the hospital bag."

"I'll call Emily to see if she can come over for Drew." He pulls his phone out of his pocket and quickly leaves the room to get the bag.

I need to let Bree know.

Where's my phone?

Lucy searches for her phone frantically. Allen comes back into the room to finish packing his last-minute items.

"I can't find my phone!"

"Luce," he says with measured calm. "It's here."

He picks it up off the bed and hands it to her. Despite his even tone, she sees his eyes are glassy with nerves. She feels her own panic increase.

"I need to tell Bree we're leaving now and that she may need to watch Drew a few extra nights."

"I'll do it, hun. Why don't you go say goodbye to Drew while I finish here?"

Lucy tries to slow her breathing as she walks down the hallway to Drew's room. The door to his room creaks and she sees his eyes peek open.

"Hi, Mama," he says sleepily.

She kisses his forehead and rubs his back. "Good morning, buddy."

He sits up and crawls into her lap. His blankets lay strewn across his bed, and she tries to smooth his unruly hair.

She hears Emily's voice downstairs. More tightening.

Eight minutes now.

"You're going to spend a little time with Ms. Emily. Mom and Dad have to go away for a night or two, but we'll be home soon. Aunt Bree will come over for a sleepover too, okay?"

"Can we build a blankie fort?"

"I bet she'd love that."

Lucy carries Drew on her hip carefully as she takes him to the living room.

She gives him a tight squeeze. "I love you, buddy. So much." His arms wrap around her neck, and she breathes in his familiar morning scent- a mixture of his lavender bedtime lotion and the faintest trace of maple syrup from yesterday's breakfast. They walk through the doorway, and she sees Emily sitting on the couch, out of breath.

"That was fast, Emily," Lucy says haltingly as another cramp starts.

"Yeah, my phone hasn't left my hand since you told me you were having contractions. When Allen called, I literally pushed Wesley to Jon and ran out the door."

As Lucy half-listens, she places her hand on the wall and closes her eyes. *Breathe.*

"You need to go!" Emily walks quickly toward her.

Lucy hugs Drew one more time before handing him to Emily. He snuggles against her chest, eyes already closing again.

Lucy leans in to give him a quick kiss on the forehead. As she does, she suddenly feels the same warmth from her flash forward at the cafe.

Everything is going to be alright.

She turns around at the doorway and smiles as she looks at her son again before walking to the car, on her way to meet her daughter.

Eloise

Two days after she quit, Eloise leaves work a few hours early after feeling especially tired all day. She had trouble falling asleep the night before and several times she felt like she was going to pass out on her keyboard.

I'm probably just tired and worn out. It's not like I'm growing an actual human being or anything.

More concerning was the blackness that clouded her vision occasionally, though. She tried calling the doctor's office, but no one answered and they hadn't returned her call. She couldn't afford calling an ambulance and she felt weird asking her boss for help. Eloise would have asked Sarah for a ride, but she was gone on a brief vacation.

It's not that far home... I'll just drive slow.

She passes little traffic on her way through the small town and thankfully she arrives home safely. Now she's curled up on the couch, or as curled up as her bump will allow. Her head rests on a floral embroidered throw pillow and she's covered with her great grandma's afghan.

Feeling like she has a little more energy after resting for a while, she stands up to start packing Parker's things.

The less time he spends here when he comes to get his stuff the better.

She grabs an empty box and heads to her room.

It takes twice as long as it should (*four times longer than before I was pregnant*). She has to stop every few minutes to catch her breath and now and then she feels the slightest bit dizzy.

Eloise yawns and picks up the last box. She sets it near the door, making a mental note to text Parker to come get them later.

She slowly walks to her daughter's room, stopping in the doorway to enjoy the bright sunlight falling across the soft blush walls. Even though it's been a few weeks, she can still smell the paint. A woven basket stands under the window, full of stuffed animals she received at the baby shower. Sitting on top is the crocheted bear and folded neatly so it hangs over the side is the blanket from Sarah. She glances at the rocking chair in the corner and imagines slowly rocking her baby to sleep, quietly singing lullabies and whispering loving words of comfort.

On top of the dresser is the jewelry box, and hanging on the wall above it is Eloise's drawing. She stands in front of it to admire it again. Wildflowers frame the edges. A blackbird soars across the canvas, a determined and hopeful look in its eyes. She's still surprised and proud that she was skilled enough to convey these emotions so clearly.

Eloise smiles at her hard work and for the inspiration she hopes her daughter will feel every day. Her daughter kicks her palm and she smiles.

"I'm glad you like it, baby girl." She rubs her hand lightly across her belly. "We're gonna be alright."

She winds up the jewelry box, opening it so she can listen to its song while she puts the finishing touches on the room. Her mom helped her assemble the crib over the weekend, and she grabs the freshly washed sheets off the dresser to pull them onto the mattress. The room spins slightly, and she places her hands on the dresser for support.

She tries calling the doctor's office again and still gets their voicemail.

I'll get a drink of water and lay down again.

She exits the room just as the music box slows on the chorus of "Blackbird." She walks slowly down the hallway with one hand on the wall to keep her balance and one on her rounded stomach.

Eloise reaches her bedroom, and she sinks down onto her bed, hoping she'll feel better after another short catnap. She takes a drink of tepid water from the glass by her nightstand.

As she brings her legs up onto the mattress, she feels a trickle of water run down her thigh, followed by an intense pressure. Then she feels another cramp run across her entire abdomen.

255

"Oh, no."

Her breath catches in her throat.

She grabs her phone off the nightstand and dials 911.

"911. What's your emergency?"

"My water just broke and I'm home alone. I'm only thirty-six weeks."

"Alright, ma'am. What's your name?"

"Eloise Murray."

She's so tired. The room spins faster. She hears the operator talking but can't make out any words. The phone feels enormously heavy. It slips from her hand and her world fades slowly to dark. Her last conscious thought is a whispered promise to her daughter.

We're gonna be alright, Evie.

Lucy

A whirlwind.

That's how Lucy thinks of her labor and delivery. She only remembers small pieces and there were several moments where she swore all the lights turned off in the room, covering them in darkness. What she remembers vividly is her final push, her daughter's first loud shrill cry and Allen's tear-filled eyes as he kissed Lucy's sweaty forehead.

I'm so thankful everything was okay, for both of us.

Lucy sits in the hospital room alone with her daughter for the first time. Allen left a few minutes ago to eat a late lunch and to make some phone calls to family members. She tucks some stray hairs behind her ear, allowing the rest to fall loosely around her shoulders. She gazes at their daughter sleeping peacefully in the crib beside her. Lucy listens to her newborn's rapid breathing, watching her chest rise and fall quickly as she learns how to breathe on her own.

She sees the stack of papers sitting on the nightstand. She reaches for the pile and then wheels the bed tray closer to write on it. The top page is the birth certificate form, and she begins filling it out. Lucy smiles as she writes her daughter's name in the first box, Evie. She thinks of all those months that went by when she hoped for and imagined this very moment. She stares at her daughter's perfectly scrunchy face, blinking back the sting of happy tears.

Sweet little, Evie.

It fits her perfectly.

Still smiling, she returns to the paperwork in front of her to complete her information next. Under the box Mother Maiden Name, Lucy writes her birth name, "Eloise Catherine Murray."

Evie stirs and fusses unhappily.

Lucy sets the pen and clipboard back and reaches into the crib beside her bed, wincing slightly with the effort.

"It's okay. Sssh. Mama's here."

She looks down at the tiny bundle in her arms while emotions flood over her. One feeling rises above the rest though, love.

She snuggles her daughter close. As warm, unchecked tears fall softly down Lucy's cheeks, she finally feels a part of herself settle firmly into place. It's a part that should have been so obvious, but that she never even realized was missing until it was suddenly there.

She smiles down at the precious bundle in her arms and whispers, "I love you, Evie."

Lucy hums the beginning of a song. She whisper-sings the chorus aloud as her daughter opens her eyes and turns her head, searching for her mother's familiar voice.

"Blackbird fly…"

Acknowledgments

Endless thanks to…

My husband for always supporting me and helping me reach this dream.

My sister for being my first reader and biggest cheerleader.

My editors, Katherine Ervin at Goblin Fruit LLC and Amber K. Cox at Better Than an Editor LLC, for making these characters real and writing them richer stories

My author friend, J.L. Hyde, for patiently answering my thousands of writing and self-publishing questions.

My ARC and review team for taking a chance on my debut book and giving me honest feedback.

My readers for choosing to spend time in these pages.

And finally to…

My children for inspiring me to take scary but beautiful risks.

Thank you all.

About the Author

Jess A. Mielbick lives in Michigan with her husband and children. If she isn't writing, reading, or getting her kids their one-hundredth snack for the day, she's roasting coffee beans for La Belle Vie Coffee. Purchase her books and coffee at www.organically-crafted.com, including her exclusive book-inspired roasts.

www.ingramcontent.com/pod-product-compliance
Lightning Source LLC
Chambersburg PA
CBHW050155120726
47903CB00002B/628